"I want you, E
now and I w
want me, too."

"I want you, Sam," she said. "But I don't know what you want out of this."

He knew exactly what she meant. They were each so emotionally raw in their own ways.

"I don't know, either," he admitted. "But I know I've felt alone and empty for too long. I think you know how that feels. I think we can make that emptiness go away, for a while, together. We deserve that, don't we?"

"And in the morning?" she asked. "What then?"

"I won't think any less of you, Erin. I haven't been able to get you out of my mind since we kissed last week. I know you felt something then, just as I did. You even said it was what was right for us at the time. And so is this."

New-Zealand-born, to Dutch immigrant parents, **Yvonne Lindsay** became an avid romance reader at the age of thirteen. Now, married to her 'blind date', and with two fabulous children, she remains a firm believer in the power of romance. Yvonne feels privileged to be able to bring to her readers the stories of her heart. In her spare time, when not writing, she can be found with her nose firmly in a book, reliving the power of love in all walks of life.

She can be contacted via her website: www.yvonnelindsay.com

Recent titles by the same author:

A FORBIDDEN AFFAIR
THE WAYWARD SON
THE PREGNANCY CONTRACT

Did you know these are also available as eBooks?
Visit www.millsandboon.co.uk

A FATHER'S SECRET

BY
YVONNE LINDSAY

MILLS & BOON

First published in Great Britain 2013
by Mills & Boon, an imprint of Harlequin (UK) Limited.
Harlequin (UK) Limited, Eton House, 18-24 Paradise Road,
Richmond, Surrey TW9 1SR

© Dolce Vita Trust 2012

ISBN: 978 0 263 90019 4

Harlequin (UK) policy is to use papers that are natural, renewable and recyclable products and made from wood grown in sustainable forests. The logging and manufacturing process conform to the legal environmental regulations of the country of origin.

Printed and bound in Spain
by Blackprint CPI, Barcelona

A FATHER'S
SECRET

To Toni Kenyon, with grateful thanks for her research in all matters relating to NZ law and this story, even though we had to transplant to another country in the end! :-)

One

"What are you going to do?"

Erin looked from the worried face of her friend to the letter in her hand and shook her head. "I don't know what I *can* do."

"You have to find out more. At least then you'll be better informed if you have to fight it," Sasha said vehemently. "What did that letter the other day say? That someone had come forward to say mistakes had been made at the fertility clinic? And with nothing to back up their claims? Seriously, it could just be a disgruntled employee creating trouble."

"Well," Erin said, waving the letter she'd received from a San Francisco law firm out of reach of her baby son's grip. "Clearly someone believes in it enough to follow it up. And besides, if it's true, if the tests prove Riley isn't James's son, do I have any *right* to fight it?"

"You're his mother, aren't you? You have every right

under the sun. This *Party A*—" Sasha sneered over the moniker "—is no more than a donor."

"Sash, really? That's a bit harsh. The man and his wife were obviously going through the clinic for the same reason James and I were. I think it's a bit cruel to say he's no more than a donor."

Erin pressed a kiss onto Riley's head, inhaling his special baby smell and relishing anew the wonder of the life she held on her lap.

Sasha had the grace to look shamefaced. "Well, either way, you're Riley's mother. No one can deny you that, and it means the odds regarding custody are firmly stacked in your favor."

It was little comfort, Erin thought as she studied the letter again. She hoped to see something, anything, that would give her some recourse to refuse to submit Riley to a DNA test to prove exactly who his father was—her late husband James or some stranger. She adjusted Riley on her lap as her heart constricted painfully. The whole situation was impossible. Riley had to be James's son. He just *had* to be. Their security hinged on it.

Mistakes like what they'd suggested simply weren't supposed to happen. When she and James had won the IVF lottery, which had taken them from their Lake Tahoe home to San Francisco to complete the procedures that led to baby Riley's birth four months ago, they'd never for one moment thought that the fertility clinic could make such a terrible mistake. Nor had either of them dreamed that the flulike symptoms James had experienced months later masked a bacterial infection—one that led to the congestive heart failure that had taken his life within two weeks of Riley's birth.

She was now left to deal with this all on her own, and the reality of it threatened to overwhelm her completely. The sheet of paper in her hand trembled and she set it down on the well-used kitchen table in front of her—a table that had been used by generations of Connells. A table that could only be used by *future* generations of Connells, according to the terms of the estate's trust. She'd thought that everything about her home was Riley's by right, as James's son. What if she was wrong? She smoothed the letter onto the worn surface and wished to God she'd never gone to the post office to collect her mail today—or ever, for that matter.

Sasha's hand came to rest on top of hers. "Don't worry, Erin. Riley's your son, nothing can change that, no matter who his father is. Write back and request more information before you'll agree to any testing. Nothing in the letter you got from the lawyers acting for the clinic has even been substantiated. It's not as if they've sent you categorical proof that a mix-up happened at all—and this letter from the lawyers acting for the other guy is couched in terms of a *request,* not a court ordered *demand.*"

Erin felt her heart lift at Sasha's suggestion. "You're right. And, at least if I write to them, that'll delay things a little longer, won't it?"

"Atta girl." Sasha looked at the kitchen clock and sighed. "Sorry, I have to go. School's out soon."

"You go, get your kids. Don't worry about me. And thanks for coming over when I lost it before."

Erin had been a trembling wreck when she'd read her mail. One call to Sasha had been all it took for her one true friend to drop everything to be by her side. In a world that had changed so dramatically over the past twelve months, having her friend's constant and loving support had been a godsend.

"Hey, that's what friends are for, right? Call me when

you get any more news, okay?" Sasha gave her a quick hug. "What time is your guest due to arrive?"

"Not until five."

"At least having a paying guest again will help out a bit financially. I still can't believe that James didn't leave you and Riley better provided for."

Erin frowned at the censure in her friend's voice. "He did his best, Sash. Neither of us ever expected he'd die so young. Plus, our medical bills after Riley's birth and James's illness—well, you know they pretty much cleaned us out."

"I know, I'm sorry, it's just so unfair..."

Erin swallowed against the lump in her throat. Yes, it was so unfair. After all they'd been through, all they'd survived. Erin felt the old familiar depression begin to creep back in and she gave herself a swift mental shake. Dwelling on the past changed nothing. She had Riley, and that was all she needed to focus on now.

After seeing Sasha off, Erin changed Riley's diaper before nursing him and putting him down for his afternoon sleep. Once he was down, she grabbed the baby monitor so she could hear if he didn't settle, and quickly went upstairs to check on the room for her new guest. It had been ages since they'd taken guests at Connell Lodge, and she was still suffering from pretty hefty doses of baby brain. She wouldn't put it past herself to have forgotten something important.

But no. The room was perfect and, with the afternoon sun streaming through the steel-paned windows, welcoming. Fresh lavender-scented linens graced the wide bed, a selection of roses from the garden, casually arranged in a crystal vase, decorated the tallboy against the wall, and the wide-plank flooring gleamed with polish. The en suite bathroom was equally pristine, with fresh towels on the rail all thick and fluffy, and a newly dry-cleaned robe on a hanger behind the door with its belt neatly knotted. Soaps, shampoos, yes, everything was there in abundance.

She'd arranged for the room across the hall from this one to be converted into a study at her guest's request. He was, apparently, working on a book and had expressed a desire for privacy during his stay. Well, there'd be no problem with that, Erin conceded. He would be the one and only visitor here for the duration. In fact, he would be the first visitor she'd had here in months. His enquiry through their website had come at just the right time.

She'd missed this—the pride in getting a room ready for guests, wondering what they'd be like, whether they'd return. It was good to be getting back to business. During James's illness they'd stopped taking guests and let their staff go. It had been too much for her to handle—being pregnant, caring for James, and having to look after everything on her own.

Erin mentally ran through her checklist and gauged what she had still to do before five o'clock. Yep, despite her mini-breakdown over the mail, she was still on track. And, provided the guest was punctual, she'd have time to get him settled in, and his evening meal warmed and served, before Riley woke for his feeding, playtime and bath. As she made her way back downstairs, her feet cushioned by the ornate carpet runner that snaked from top to bottom, she found herself feeling happy for the first time in a long time. Maybe things were starting to look up after all.

Sam Thornton let himself out of the car and gasped a little at the old familiar pain in his right leg and hip.

Sitting for as long as he had during the four-plus hour drive from San Francisco certainly hadn't done his frustratingly slow-to-heal body any favors. He should have flown into Reno, but then he would have been stuck with a driver he neither knew nor trusted. So Sam had convinced himself he was better off being driven the whole distance. He straightened, breathing through the pain and slowly stretching out his muscles.

"You all right, sir?" his driver asked, coming around the side of the car.

"I'll be fine, Ray, thanks. I should have listened to you and let you stop more often along the way—for your sake if not for mine."

Ray cocked an eyebrow. "Was that an admission of fault, sir?"

"You know it was, now shut up and help me with my bag." Sam smiled to take any sting from his words. It didn't matter, though. Even when Sam had been at his worst, and there'd been many days like that, Ray had merely endured whatever his irritable boss had flung at him and carried on doing his job. After all they'd weathered together, Sam considered Ray a friend as much as an employee—and he was silently grateful to have a friend with him at this particular moment as he braced himself for what he was about to do.

Sam looked at the imposing old English-style country house ahead of him. Two-storied, the concrete stucco exterior hosted multiple vines of some kind of creeper. The growth was a little unkempt, as if it hadn't been pruned in a while. In fact, the whole property had the air of something beginning a slow, inexorable slide into neglect.

He shook his head slightly. It wasn't the house that interested him, and he couldn't care less about how well it was maintained. He was here with a far more important agenda.

"Are you sure you don't want me to stay with you for a day or two, sir?" Ray asked as he handed Sam his bag and laptop case.

"I don't need babysitting," Sam responded, a little sharply. He closed his eyes a moment and sighed. "I'm sorry, Ray. What I meant to say is, no, thank you. I'll be fine. You head on off and go vacation at your daughter's as you arranged. I'll call you when I need you. Hopefully that won't be for a while."

"Sure thing."

Ray gave him a nod, then climbed back into the sleek black Audi A6. He guided the car around the circle of the drive and out onto the road. Alone now in the driveway, Sam knew there was no going back. He bent to pick up his bag and started to walk toward the lodge just as a tall, slender woman with short dark hair opened the wide front door and stepped out onto the shaded portico.

The private investigator he'd hired to track her down had failed to mention just how attractive the young widow was.

"Good afternoon," she said, "Welcome to Connell Lodge. You must be Mr. Thornton."

Sam stopped in his tracks. His hand gripped the handle of his carry bag so tightly it made his knuckles ache. This wasn't happening. He was not attracted to this woman—he wasn't allowed to be. He pushed against the hot thud of desire that beat through his veins, hard. But his body, traitorous thing that it was, was on fire. Flames licked through parts of his physique that he'd ignored now for so long that he thought he'd grown numb. Welcomingly numb.

"Mr. Thornton?"

He was caught by the worried look in her eyes—eyes that were a chocolate-brown so deep a man could get lost inside their depths and never care. He gave himself a swift mental shake. He was *not* attracted to this woman. Not on any level. He would not allow it.

"Yes, I'm Sam Thornton. Please, call me Sam."

He stepped forward, his gait still uneven after his car journey, and held out his hand.

"I'm Erin, Erin Connell, your hostess."

She took his hand in hers, and in that instant he knew he'd lost his battle with himself. A sizzle of awareness started at the point where their palms met and shot up his arm. To his surprise, she uttered a small "Oh!" before releasing his hand and taking a step back. So she was affected, too. *Great. Bloody great,* he thought dourly. This should not be happening.

"Please, come inside and let me show you your room," she said, her voice a little huskier than it had been before. "Can I help you with your things?"

"No, I'll manage on my own, thanks."

She turned and preceded him into the lodge, affording him an excellent view of her rigid spine and the way it led in a straight line to the gentle arcs of her hips and bottom. Hips and bottom that were firmly clad in white denim that would probably be outlawed in some countries for the way it clung to her curves. Another clench of desire hit him hard and low and he forced himself to breathe through it.

This was insane. Erin Connell wasn't even his type, he thought, as he followed her up the old wooden staircase to the next floor. He didn't have a type. Didn't want one, ever again. And yet, despite his silent protestations, there was still that nagging interest.

"Are you visiting from overseas?" she asked.

He got that a lot. "No, I'm from New Zealand originally, but I've been based in the States for about eight years now."

"Oh, really? I've always wanted to go there. I hear it's beautiful. Maybe one day," she said airily as they reached the top of the stairs.

He was relieved not to have her enticing shape smack bang in his line of vision any longer. He followed her a short distance along the carpeted corridor and into a large, well-lit room that faced formal gardens to the rear of the property. Well, he supposed they must have been formal once. Again, there was that sense of neglect. He looked around the room. Whatever neglect there was outdoors, it didn't extend to the inside.

"This is your room. I'm sure you'll find you have everything you need here," she said, moving through the space and across to open another door that clearly led to his private bathroom. "But if there's anything else you require, please don't hesitate to let me know."

Her smile faltered as he stood there, just staring at her like an idiot. He forced himself to make some sound of approval and clearly he succeeded because her features relaxed once more.

"Now, you asked for an office also, so I've created space for you across the hall from your room. If you'll come this way?"

He followed her directly across the hall to a wood-paneled room, with a desk situated near a deep window that looked out across the private bay and beyond to the lake.

"I thought you might like the lake view while you're working," she continued. "I hope that's all right?"

"It's great," he answered. And it was, even if he

couldn't quite infuse his voice with the right level of gratitude. For what little she was charging, he'd have been grateful for a broom cupboard under the stairs. He made a mental note to ensure he paid her a generous bonus for the effort she'd clearly gone to for him, although he doubted she'd accept it when she found out exactly why he was here. "Thank you."

She gave him another of those smiles that hit him square in the gut. "You're welcome. We…well, I aim to please," she said, her voice a little shaky. "I'll leave you to unpack your things. You mentioned in your booking email that you'd prefer to dine early, so I have your dinner warming in the oven downstairs. The dining room is directly opposite the bottom of the stairs on the ground floor and you'll find a bellpull just inside the door. Please ring for me when you're ready."

"Thank you, but you don't have to wait on me hand and foot, Erin."

Her name felt foreign on his tongue, and yet weirdly right at the same time. Had this place cast some strange spell upon him, he wondered, then thrust the random thought away for the foolishness it was. No, there was no spell. If anything, his crazy and sudden attraction to Erin Connell probably had its roots in something older and more primitive. Something that had little to do with sex itself, or the unwelcome raw need he felt for her, and everything to do with the fact he believed she was the woman who had borne his son.

Two

Sam's eyes lit upon the monitor she had clipped to her belt, and he felt a strange tightness in his chest. As if on cue, the machine squawked into life and Sam heard his child's cry for the very first time. He blinked back the sudden moisture that burned at his eyes and swallowed against the lump in his throat, forcing himself to speak.

"Your baby?" he asked, his voice remarkably level despite his churning emotions.

"Yes, my son. He's four months old, but you don't need to worry that he'll disturb you while you're here. We live downstairs at the opposite end of the lodge and he's now sleeping through the night, thank goodness."

"It's no problem." He dredged up a smile. "Don't hide him away on my account." The noise through the monitor grew more demanding. "It sounds like you're being summoned. Don't let me hold you up."

"Thanks," Erin said, already heading for the door.

"Remember to just ring for me when you're ready for your meal. I'll bring it straight through."

Sam raised his hand in acknowledgment and watched as she rapidly left the room. He expelled a harsh breath and turned to face the window, staring wildly out onto the serene surface of the lake and waiting in vain for it to fill him with a sense of calm that he hadn't felt in far too long. It had been an entire year since his wife's death. A year filled with pain, loss, grief and over-whelming guilt. He'd welcomed each one and borne it stoically. It was the least he could do, considering it was a stupid decision on his part that had taken Laura's life.

He'd vowed he'd never enter into another relation-ship with anyone—ever. He'd even had a vasectomy to ensure that he couldn't screw up another person's life again. He owed Laura and her memory that much. Up until today, that hadn't been a problem, but there was something about his hostess that pinged every single one of his male receptors. Knowing that Erin Connell had that effect on him angered and scared him in equal quotients. Not even with his beautiful wife had attrac-tion been so raw, so intense, so instant.

So very, very wrong, especially since he was only at Lake Tahoe to do something she'd probably consider unforgivable. He'd come to find a way to claim her son.

Erin all but ran to the back stairs that would take her down to her living quarters. Wow, that guy was intense. Not to mention a whole lot younger and way more attractive than she'd counted on for her first guest since reopening. She unconsciously wiped her right hand against her hip, trying to assuage the tingle that had started with his handshake and spread through her whole body every time he'd looked at her.

She pattered down the stairs and let herself into her quarters, heading straight toward Riley's nursery and the little hands that waved above the edge of his crib for her attention. Scooping her son up against her shoulder she automatically began to rock and make the soothing sounds she knew would settle him and tried not to wince as his strong fists closed in her hair.

"Hey, little man," she crooned. "Did you have a nice nap? It wasn't quite long enough, though, was it? Did you hear our new visitor arrive? Is that what it is? Are you afraid you're missing out on something, hmm?"

Erin carried Riley through to his room and placed him on the changing table, whipping off his wet diaper and replacing it with a dexterity she'd once doubted she'd ever manage. As she did so, she kept up a running commentary.

"I don't blame you for wanting to meet our Mr. Thornton. He's a bit of a hottie, not that I was looking, mind you. Only one man in my life," she said bending down to blow a raspberry on Riley's little belly. "And that's you!"

She lifted Riley back up again as his chortles of glee faded away, striving to keep her focus where it belonged—squarely on her son. But meeting Sam Thornton had completely shaken her equilibrium. He was nothing like his courteously friendly emails had implied. She'd expected someone older, someone…well, duller. Not sex on legs.

His dark blond hair was cropped short and there were lines on his forehead and bracketing the sides of his mouth that suggested laughter was not something that came frequently to him. But his slate-gray eyes had been mesmerizing. She'd felt as if he could look right through her, to her very soul, if he so desired. And then there was his touch.

She shivered and clutched Riley just a little too tightly in reaction, earning a squeak of protest from her son. No, she didn't want to go there, even though it had been a very long time since anyone had made her feel like that. All woman, all the way.

Erin made her way through to the kitchen and propped Riley in the tabletop rocker that gave him a clear line of sight for whatever she was doing. She adjusted the small toy mobile that was attached to one side so he could grab and play with it if he got bored watching her. She hummed a tune while she laid a large butler's tray with all the condiments she thought her guest would enjoy with the casserole of braised beef and red wine she'd prepared earlier in the day and that now stood warming in the oven.

She'd made enough that she could freeze a couple of single portions for future meals for herself. With creamy mashed potatoes and fresh green vegetables from the kitchen garden, it would be a hearty meal. Perhaps too hearty, given that it was still late summer and the evenings were still long and, so far, delightfully warm.

She gave a mental shrug. If he had any complaints he could bring them to the management, she thought with a smile—the management that began and ended with her. It was a daunting enough role at the best of times, but Erin loved Connell Lodge with a passion. Arriving here for an interview to join the—then—much larger household staff, she'd felt as if she'd found home for the very first time in her life. She had come here with nothing and had made a life, created a family and a sense of belonging.

Ten years later, that home was being challenged by

some stranger's assertion that Riley was not her husband's son. *Party A,* whoever he was, had no idea what can of worms he'd upended.

Legal advice, that was what she needed. But legal advice came with a price tag that she wasn't in a position to pay, and she wasn't about to use the firm that had handled the Connell family affairs for over a hundred years. Not when they were the very people who'd see her and Riley removed from the property if this whole paternity business didn't go away.

She shook her head. She'd been James's wife in every meaning of the word. Riley was their son. Connell Lodge was Riley's home for his lifetime. The archaic trust that held the property only allowed direct descendants of the original James Connell, who built the property back in the early 1900s, to live there. As James's legal and biological son, Riley and she—as his mother—had every right to be there.

A chill of foreboding ran down her spine. But what if a mistake had been made?

God, she hated this whole situation and the horribly vulnerable position it had put her in. If she had to leave right now, all she and Riley would have were the clothes on their backs and the very small amount of money left in her bank account. She had no skills other than being darn good at keeping the lodge in order and providing for their guests, and while she could competently skipper the boat moored at the end of the private pier, their charter license had long since lapsed. James had been the great outdoorsman, not to mention a much sought-after fishing guide, while all she'd ever wanted was a home—and Connell Lodge was that home.

Losing the very roof over her head was not an option. Somehow, she had to get the proof she needed to make this all go away.

A name popped into her head. Janet Morin. She'd met Janet during childbirth classes and knew the other woman had planned to return part-time to her legal practice in South Lake Tahoe almost immediately after the birth of her daughter. Maybe she could help, or at least be able to advise Erin on the best route to take without costing a small fortune. She'd make enquiries in the next few days, sound the woman out. She certainly didn't want a whiff of any of this getting to the trustees who handled Connell Lodge—at least, not before she knew exactly where she stood, however shaky that ground may be.

Riley chose that moment to bump his nose with the toy he'd been clutching in his fist and sent up an almighty wail of protest. She unbuckled him from the rocker and lifted him in her arms but he was determined to be inconsolable.

"Shh, Riley-bear, shh," she murmured as she held him close and peppered his little face with kisses, but he wasn't having any of it.

From experience she knew there was only one way to soothe him. With one eye on the old-fashioned board, decorated with bells that were connected to the main rooms, she settled in a kitchen chair, unbuttoned the top of her blouse and adjusted her clothing so he could nurse. Riley latched onto her with gusto, and Erin wiped his chubby little cheeks of the tears that had stained them.

"Oh, Riley, your timing is kind of off, sweetheart. Our guest is going to be down for his dinner soon and I don't think he'll be impressed with me bringing along his meal with you attached to me like this."

"I'm happy to wait."

The voice from the door made her start, popping Riley off her. She swiftly guided him back and arranged her blouse a little more modestly.

"I'm sorry," she said, color flaring in her cheeks as she saw exactly where Sam Thornton's eyes were locked. "I didn't hear you ring for me."

"I didn't." Sam limped the rest of the way into the kitchen and pulled out a chair at the table. "I went to the dining room, and while it's a beautiful room, the idea of eating there alone didn't really suit. Do you mind if I eat here, with you?"

Did she mind? Part of her yelled, *"Hell, yes!"* But there was an entreaty in his voice, a loneliness that struck her to her core. Did that explain the shadows in his eyes? The lines drawn on his handsome face?

"No, I don't mind at all," she said as smoothly as she could. "I'm sorry, about this. Riley's a bit out of his usual routine for some reason. Maybe he's heading for another growth spurt."

"Riley? That's his name?"

She must be hearing things. Was that wistfulness in Sam Thornton's voice?

"Sure is," she replied, swiftly covering up as Riley disengaged from her and turned to give a milky smile to the newcomer. "Riley James Connell, at your service."

"May I hold him?"

Erin couldn't quite disguise her shock. He wanted to hold Riley? In her experience, most men ran a mile from kids at this age, preferring them when they were older, toilet trained and at least partly able to conduct a conversation. "Most men" being her late husband, that is.

"Sure, I'll just need to burp him first," she said, fix-

ing her clothing with one hand and propping Riley up-
right on her lap with the other.

"I can do that," Sam said.

"You've done it before?" she asked in surprise.

"No, but how hard can it be?"

The man didn't know what he was in for. "He still
sometimes spits up a bit when he burps."

"So put a towel on my shoulder," Sam said nonchalantly. "That is what you do, isn't it?"

Erin nodded and rose, getting a small towel from a
kitchen drawer and giving it to him. He laid it over his
shoulder and then held his hands out for Riley, who
happily went into the arms of the stranger.

She was unable to tear her gaze from her baby in
this man's embrace. "He'll be more comfortable if you
hold him like so." She guided one of Sam's arms under
Riley's diapered bottom. "And if you rub his back with
your other hand, holding him against you."

Sam did as she suggested. It looked wrong, and yet
right at the same time, and it reminded her that Riley
had missed out on a lot of male contact with his father
gone. But should he be getting that contact with Sam
Thornton? She didn't even know the man, yet somehow
she instinctively felt she could trust him. When Riley
belched, Sam's face took on a look of pride that made
her laugh out loud. You'd have thought it was Sam himself who'd created the hearty sound.

"Wow, the boy can burp," he said, still gently rubbing the baby's back.

"And that's not all," Erin said, a smile still wreathing
her face. "You should see what he does at the other end."

A look of horror passed over Sam's features. "I can
just imagine. Here, do you want him back?"

"No, I'll finish getting our meal together. You can

put him back in his rocker if you don't want to keep holding him."

"Is it safe?" Sam said, looking at the rocker.

"Sure, and it's a huge help. Short of having him strapped to me during his waking hours, it's a great way for him to be a bit independent of me and still see what I'm doing around the place."

"It's okay," he said, "I'll hold him until we're ready to eat."

Erin grabbed a second place setting and laid the kitchen table for the two of them. Even with Riley there, it felt strangely intimate to be laying the table for two. The last time she'd done this it had been several months ago, while James was still well enough to leave his bed and come to the kitchen. She pushed the memories aside. She didn't want to go there right now. She had more than enough to think about.

Sam held the tiny body in his arms and fought to swallow past the lump in his throat. As hard as it was to believe, he could actually be holding his son. Every instinct in his body wanted to hold this child to him and protect him from the ravages of the world, but he had no right to do that until he knew for certain that Riley was his.

He watched Erin as she competently moved through the kitchen, transforming a bare table to a convivial setting with effortless ease. The aroma of the dish she'd removed from the oven to stand on a trivet on the table spoke volumes to her ability as a cook. Even now, his mouth was watering. It all seemed to come so easily to her and reminded him uncomfortably of how natural she'd been with Riley when he'd entered the kitchen, following the sounds of the baby's cries.

Seeing the baby at her breast had brought home a whole new range of emotions. Erin offered sustenance to her son from her own body. It was perfectly natural, and yet he'd never even stopped to think about the baby's level of dependence upon her as his mother. He wondered if Laura would have been the same—if she'd have nursed their child. They'd never even taken their discussions that far. Instead, their focus had just been on the business of getting pregnant. That focus had been consuming to the point of excluding almost everything else.

Guilt swamped him anew, making him feel disloyal to his late wife's memory. It seemed like a betrayal to Laura to be here, to be holding this child who might be *his* but not *theirs*. To be watching Erin Connell and not Laura. If he'd only been on time to pick Laura up for their appointment instead of insisting on attending to just one more issue that had cropped up at the office. One more issue that he'd since been forced, by his injuries, to learn to delegate. But it was far too late now. Too late for Laura and too late for the child conceived for them at the fertility center.

Even surrogacy was out of the question. As far as he knew, their viable embryos had been destroyed in the clinic failure that had resulted when several anomalies had been discovered in their business practices. Anger licked at the edges of his mind. A wasted emotion now, he knew. But, according to clinic records, one of those mistakes could mean that this child in his arms had been conceived with his sperm.

"Everything okay?"

Erin's voice broke through his reverie, jolting him free of the pain of the past and dragging him, all too

willingly, into her company and the warmth and welcome of her kitchen.

"Yeah, I'm fine. That smells great." He nodded in
the direction of the table.

"You didn't specify any dietary requirements, so I
hope this will be okay."

She ducked her head shyly, making him realize he'd
been staring at her for far longer than was probably po-
lite. Erin took Riley from him and settled the child in
his rocker, where he played and gurgled happily while
they sat at the table.

"This is incredible," Sam said as he tasted the casserole she'd ladled generously onto his plate. "Where
did you train?"

"Train?"

"To cook like this." He lifted another piece of suc-
culent and richly flavored beef to his mouth.

She initially said nothing, just watched as he ate. For
some reason, having her watch him wasn't uncomfortable, unless you counted the state of semi-arousal he'd
been in from the moment he'd arrived here.

She averted her eyes from his face and focused instead on her plate. "I'm self-taught, pretty much. Connell Lodge had a cook here when I arrived, but she
preferred plain food without much seasoning. I started
to experiment with a few dishes, and when she retired
soon after I got here James offered me the cook's role
full-time."

"You were staff here?" That was something that
hadn't been in the dossier his private investigator had
put together for him. Mind you, the man had barely had
a week to gather information about her, and at Sam's
insistence was still on a quest for more.

"Initially, yes." A bittersweet smile crossed her face. "I was a bit of a cliché, really—marrying the boss."

A sharp pang of envy lanced through him. Sam pushed it away ruthlessly. He had no right to feel any envy for the relationship Erin had enjoyed with her husband. He himself had been very happily married—hadn't even so much as looked at another woman in the years he and Laura had been together, and in the aftermath of her death, he'd sworn he never would again.

Erin continued. "The rest, as they say, is history."

"So, what brought you here in the first place?" He was keen to fill the gaps in what little he knew of her past.

"I applied for work—general house duties. It was heading into winter and one of their regulars had fallen and broken her leg, leaving them short staffed. I was staying at a hostel about half an hour from here and saw a notice in the local paper, so I hitched out and applied for the job."

"And never left," he commented. "What did you do before you came here?"

Her expression changed, the friendliness in her eyes disappearing as effectively as if he'd just stolen her most precious possession. And, he suddenly realized, wasn't that what he was here to do, after all?

"Oh, a bit of this and a bit of that," she answered evasively. "Nothing important."

Clearly, she didn't like to talk about her past. More, he had the instinctive sensation that she was hiding something there that she would rather not have brought into the open. That instinct was what had led him to be where he was today. It had driven him to the top of his field in software development because he was never satisfied with simple answers. It made him all the more determined to discover everything he could about her. This irrational attraction toward her aside, he found he needed to know whatever it was that Erin Connell was hiding. Any secret could be a weapon to get him his son.

Three

Erin carefully sealed the envelope addressed to the San Francisco city law firm acting for Party A. Inside it was her very cautiously worded letter in which she requested more information to support Party A's request. She could only hope that the mail would take several days to reach them, even though deep down she knew it probably wouldn't take more than a few.

The past couple of days had made it easy to put the whole matter out of her head. She had been busy taking care of her guest—keeping his rooms tidy and clean, providing his meals for him and shamelessly enjoying his male company while she did so. And then there was Riley, who was growing and changing daily—she could hear him gurgling happily through the monitor on her hip. She'd left him on his play mat in her sitting room while she dashed to the office to get the envelope.

Yes, it was a busy life and she loved it. She didn't want to lose it.

She had an appointment in South Lake Tahoe mid-morning with Janet Morin to see if she could get a better idea of where she stood in this whole business. Janet had been more than happy to make time to see Erin when she'd called and loosely explained her situation. The woman said she'd be happy to advise, pro bono, and Erin's relief had been palpable. Now, something that had filled her with dread was not so scary after all.

Erin started to put the envelope in her handbag and turned to leave the small office she'd adopted as her own when she'd taken over the administration side of running Connell Lodge a couple of years ago. She walked straight into the solid wall of male muscle that was Sam Thornton—her bag and its contents flying in one direction, the envelope in the other.

She reached out to steady herself, her hands coming to rest on a broad expanse of chest, the fine cotton of Sam's shirt doing little to hide the definition of lean muscle behind it. At the same time, strong warm fingers closed around her upper arms. She could smell the clean scent of him, the slightly spicy tang of his cologne a subtle fragrance that was purely male and as intoxicating as hell.

Her breathing became uneven as she looked up into his eyes—eyes that were dark and stormy and bored straight back into her own. For a crazy second, Erin almost thought he was going to kiss her. The thought filled her with both terror and intrigue. What would he taste like, how would his lips feel on hers? And then the moment was gone. Sam's eyes became cooler, remote, and he gently set her away from him and took a step back from her. She must have been imagining things. Maybe even wanting things a little too much. She forced herself to look away and bent to collect the scattered contents of her bag just as Sam did the same.

"Sorry," she said, her voice a little rough around the edges. "I was distracted. I didn't see you."

"No, it's my fault, I should have knocked before coming in."

His long-fingered hands closed over the envelope and Erin saw him hesitate a moment before passing it to her. Sam was from San Francisco. Did he recognize the name of the firm on the front of the envelope? Did he wonder what she was doing sending mail to them? She gave herself a mental shake. What would he care anyway? Whatever her legal business, it had nothing to do with him.

She finished stuffing her things into her bag and rose to her feet, suddenly very aware of Sam and of how close he now stood.

"D-did you want me for something?" she stuttered, drawing in another breath of his essence before stepping backward.

"I need to print some things," he said, his stony-gray gaze never leaving her face. Did he somehow know how much he rattled her? How his very presence made her want things from him she had no right wanting or even thinking about? "I was wondering if the printer here in your office was wireless and if I could set up the drivers in my laptop so I can send to it."

The banality of his request dragged her concentration very firmly away from where it was heading. She shook her head. "I'm sorry, it's an old printer and we've never had a need for a wireless setup. I'm going into town this morning, though. I'd be happy to swing by the office supply store and pick up a printer for you to use upstairs."

Mentally she counted the cost of what getting that printer would be. Surely he wouldn't need top-of-the-line. Something basic would do and hopefully that wouldn't be too expensive.

"Why don't I come with you?" Sam suggested. "I can buy it myself and get some paper and other supplies at the same time. What time are you leaving?"

"Oh," Erin said, looking at her watch, calculating the drive into town and factoring in the change to her original plans. "Let's say in half an hour, nine o'clock. I have an appointment at ten that I can't be late for, but leaving at nine should give us time to go to the office supply store and then maybe I can drop you somewhere before I head to my meeting?"

"Don't worry about dropping me anywhere. I wouldn't want you to be late. Just leave me to get the printer and I'll wait for you near there. There must be somewhere that has a chair, a newspaper and a cup of coffee close by."

Erin felt a wave of relief. Juggling Sam around her visit to the lawyer's office could have gotten a bit messy time-wise.

"There are plenty of places that do just that. Well, if you're sure, perhaps we can leave a little after nine?"

"That'd be great," Sam nodded. "Are you bringing Riley?"

"No, not today. A friend of mine is coming here to look after him."

Sasha had jumped at the chance to babysit Riley for a couple of hours. She had also teased Erin merci-lessly about finally being forced to share her guest with someone else. Erin felt a rush of heat stain her cheeks recalling how she'd described Sam to her friend over the phone. Sasha's sudden shrieked response of "You're attracted to him!" had been an unpleasant shock. Her feelings had to be blatantly obvious if Sasha could pick up on them over the phone. She'd vehemently denied any interest in Sam, but Sasha hadn't been deterred. Erin could only hope her friend wouldn't embarrass her in front of Sam when she arrived.

"A friend? Do you trust her with Riley?" Sam's voice sounded unusually hard, almost disapproving.

"Trust Sasha?" Erin laughed. "Of course I do. I've known her for ten years and she's successfully raising three kids of her own. The youngest has just started school. Sash is my main go-to person when I need a break or can't take Riley with me when I go out. Besides, she loves him to bits. She wouldn't let any harm come to him."

The sound of a car pulling up around the back of the house warned her that Sasha was here.

"That'll be her now," Erin said. "I'd better go let her in."

Sam stood to one side as she bustled past, but not so far away that she didn't get another enticing whiff of his cologne, borne on the heat of his body. She needed to train herself to hold her breath around him, she decided irrationally. It was getting too hard to be in the same room as Sam without starting to think about things that no young widow with a baby should be thinking about.

Erin headed through the lodge and flung open the back door just as Sasha raised her hand to knock.

"How's that for timing?" Sasha said with a grin. "Now, where's my boy?"

Erin leaned forward to give her friend a quick hug before stepping back to let her through. "He's on his mat in my sitting room and is thoroughly entranced by the play gym you gave him. You spoil him, you know."

"Ah, he's easy to spoil. And how are things going with Mr. Handsome?" Sasha asked, waggling her eyebrows. "This old married lady wants to live vicariously."

Erin laughed, wondering what Sam would think of Sasha grilling her about him. "Old? I don't think so. And 'things' as you so neatly put it, are going just fine. Mr. Thornton is the perfect guest. Not a single complaint from him so far."

"And what would I have to complain about?"

Erin's cheeks flared with heat for the second time that morning. She wheeled around to see Sam leaning nonchalantly against the doorjamb that led into the kitchen. Damn it, but the man could move as silently as a ghost. Just how much had he heard? She suffered a moment of silent agony at the thought that he might have caught Sasha's moniker for him, and hoped like mad that he wouldn't have thought it had come from her.

"Nothing, I hope," she said with what she hoped was a calmness she was far from feeling on the inside.

"Of course not," Sasha interjected. "Erin's one of the best in the business. Hi, I'm Sasha Edsell."

"Sam Thornton." Sam offered his hand. "Sorry to interrupt you ladies, but I just wanted to confirm what time we're leaving?"

"About a quarter past nine, if that's okay with you?"

"Great, thanks. Nice meeting you, Sasha."

Sam excused himself to get ready, leaving the two women alone. As he disappeared from view, Erin puzzled over the way it almost seemed that he'd wanted to meet Sasha for himself, as if he hadn't believed her when she said she trusted her friend with Riley. She eschewed the idea as quickly as she thought it. It wasn't as if Sam had any say or interest in Riley's welfare beyond that of a casual observer.

Sasha fanned herself theatrically. "Oh, my, you weren't kidding when you said he was handsome. I don't blame you for taking him with you today. If you left him behind I might have been inclined to jump his bones myself!"

"Sasha, please!" Erin said, putting a finger to her lips to caution her friend to silence. Sometimes Sasha's enthusiasm for an idea was simply irrepressible and Erin couldn't fight the smile that tweaked at her lips. "Besides, Tony would never approve."

She didn't for one minute think that Sasha would cheat on her husband. Her friend was very happily married but, as she'd pointed out more than once, she wasn't blind.

"How are you going to manage with the gorgeous Sam for your trip into town?" Sasha asked as they entered the sitting room before picking Riley up for a cuddle.

"It won't be a problem. He needs some stuff from the office supply store so I'm leaving him there. It's just across the road from the lawyers. He said he'll wait for me until I'm done."

"Did you notice something familiar about him?" Sasha asked. "I feel like I've seen him somewhere before, but I can't quite put my finger on it."

"Familiar? No. Maybe you've seen him in the papers or something. I believe he's some high-flying businessman in San Francisco, but he's here on some kind of sabbatical to write a book."

"Hmm, you could be right. Ah well, it'll come to me if it's important. You should go and get yourself ready if you're going to leave on time," Sasha urged. "Riley will be just fine with me."

"Thanks, Sash," Erin said. Satisfied that Riley was in safe hands, Erin shot through to her bedroom to change her clothes and get ready.

As she dressed, she thought about how grateful she was for her friend's help. She wanted her wits about her for the meeting this morning, so not having the distraction of Riley there was a relief. Talking about the problems with the fertility clinic would be hard enough without having her beautiful, perfect son in front of her to remind her how much she stood to lose.

Sam drummed his fingers on the desk in his office, staring out at the tranquil bay beyond and wondering about the contents of the letter Erin had written to his lawyers. He knew exactly what was in the letter that had been sent to Erin, and he'd expected to have heard from his lawyer by now regarding her response. Now, it appeared she'd been dragging her feet over a reply. The knowledge that she'd been taking her time to write back when she could simply have called them on the phone or sent an email, lit a slow simmering anger inside of him.

Did she not care at all that Riley might have a living father? A man who wanted to love him and be a part of his life just as much as she was? A man who, if the tests checked out, had every right to be? A man who had denied himself the right to have a child, or even to love again, after letting down his wife so badly? That very same man was now faced with the enthralling opportunity to be a father after all, and she was stalling to keep him from it.

All it would take was a cheek swab. He'd already registered his own with the testing laboratory. This wait-

ing around felt interminable. He'd wondered already
how it would stand if he'd done the swab of Riley's
cheek himself, when she wasn't in the room, but he had
a suspicion that somewhere along the line her permission would be necessary before the legal eagles would
accept such evidence in a bid for any kind of custody.

His fingers curled into a fist of frustration, clenching
so tightly his knuckles ached. His lawyers had warned
him the process could take more time than he was willing to allow. It was part of the reason he'd hired an investigator to find her and definitely part of the reason
why he'd come here. Waiting had never come easy for
Sam. He was a results-oriented person and to get results
you had to *do* things. Still, it wasn't as if he had any
other option right now, but to wait. A glance at his watch
reminded him that it was time to head downstairs.

Erin waited for him in the lobby. As he did every
time he saw her, he felt that familiar tug of temptation
and, oh, boy, did she look tempting. She'd changed from
her usual jeans and a blouse to a simply tailored navy
dress with white piping, one that left her slender arms
bare, with a wide neckline that exposed her collarbones.
His mouth dried as he imagined tracing those delicate
hollows with the tip of his tongue. Swallowing against
the dryness and averting his eyes from examining the
rest of her body, Sam reached for the front door.

"Shall we go then?" he said.

"Yes, I'm all ready."

They walked outside to the driveway where she'd
parked the all-wheel-drive station wagon a little earlier. The car was much like the one he used to drive
before the accident, right down to the color. A cold fist
gripped his chest, making it difficult to draw a breath.
He hadn't taken the wheel of a vehicle since that fate-

ful day. In fact, Ray was the only person he'd trusted enough to drive him since the accident. Even then, it had taken several nail-biting months before he'd relaxed enough to sit in the front passenger seat.

A cold sweat broke over his body. This had been a stupid idea. He had no idea what kind of driver Erin was. She could be a speed freak for all he knew. A trickle of moisture ran down his spine.

Oblivious to what was going through his mind, Erin smiled beside him and held up a key ring, offering it to him. "Would you like to drive?"

"Hell no!" he erupted.

She looked taken aback by his short outburst but calmly palmed the keys and went around to the driver's side of the vehicle. He forced himself to take the necessary final step that would get him to the car door. His hand shook as he reached for the handle, lifting it and pulling the door open. He shouldn't have suggested he come with her. He should simply have stayed in his room and kept working. But he refused to back down now. He hadn't gotten where he was today by backing down from challenges—even if the only one challenging him was himself.

Somehow he seated himself in the passenger seat. He scrabbled for the seat belt, yanking it so swiftly the mechanism locked and failed to let him pull the belt out far enough to clip it.

"If you just let it roll back a bit," Erin suggested, giving him a strange look, "it'll let you pull it out slowly."

He gave it another tug, a hard one, and it locked again. To his surprise, Erin leaned across him, her breasts pressing against his arm as she reached around him and her hand settled over his.

"Here," she said, "like this."

He forced himself to relinquish his death grip on the seatbelt and allowed her to release the belt before pulling it smoothly across his chest and lap.

"There you go," she said securing it into the buckle. "All safe."

Safe? She was kidding right? You were only as safe as the skill set of the next idiot on the road. In his case, *he'd* been that idiot, and Laura had paid the ultimate price for his arrogance. Sam forced himself to breathe slowly—in through his nose, out through his mouth—and try to relax.

"Thanks," he said abruptly, his eyes locked on the windshield in front of him.

Erin started the car and eased it into gear, rolling slowly down the driveway. So far, so good, Sam thought, but all sense of safety fled the moment she turned onto the road. He tried to relax his grip on the door's hand rest, but he failed miserably.

"How long is the trip?" he asked, his voice sounding unnaturally strained, even to his ears.

"Twenty-five minutes or so," Erin said, her eyes flicking from the rearview mirror and back to the road in front of them again.

Twenty-five minutes. It may as well be a lifetime, Sam thought as she guided the vehicle along the winding road. He had to admit she was a competent driver, not taking any unnecessary risks or taking any of the corners too wide. He could almost kid himself that he was starting to relax until he saw a car start to pull out of a driveway ahead of them. His foot stomped an imaginary brake, the action earning him another cautious sideways glance from Erin but, thankfully, she kept her thoughts to herself.

By the time they reached the office supply store he couldn't get out of the car fast enough.

"Will you be okay if I leave you now?" Erin asked quietly as she got out of the car to stand beside him, one small hand resting on his forearm as if to offer him comfort.

"Yeah, I'll be fine, thanks," he said stoically.

"There's a café right there," she said, pointing to a bustling business not far from where she'd parked. "And I'll be just down the road. Do you want my cell number, in case you need me?"

Need her? He hadn't been able to stop wanting her since the moment he'd set foot on the soil of Connell Lodge, but need her? No, he didn't want to need anybody.

"No, seriously, I'll be fine. When you're finished just come and get me at the café. I'll buy you a coffee before we head back."

"Sure, sounds like fun," Erin said. "I won't be far, anyway," she continued, pointing to a two-story white building farther down the street.

Sam made out the signage at the front. Morin and Morin, Attorneys at Law. She was going to see a lawyer? What exactly did that mean? Was she going to try and fight his right to find out if he was Riley's father? All sorts of irrational and angry thoughts peppered his mind as he watched her head down the road and enter the building she'd indicated.

He slipped his cellphone from his pocket and hit the speed dial for his lawyer's direct line.

"Dave," he said the moment he heard the man's voice on the end of the phone. "I want you to get a court order to request the baby's DNA, now."

"Good morning to you, too, Sam," David Fox's

amused voice echoed in his ear. "I thought we decided on a softer approach first time around, to gauge if the other party would enter discussions and testing willingly. You know, avoid potentially antagonizing the woman who might just be your baby's mother? The woman you probably don't really want to alienate?"

"I know," Sam said, huffing out a breath of frustration. "But I don't want to wait any longer. I want the tests done and I want those answers now."

"I'll see what I can do," the lawyer replied, his voice now all solemnity. Maybe he finally understood how serious Sam was.

"Good, call me when you have news."

Sam disconnected the call and shoved the phone back in his pocket. So, Erin Connell thought she could fight him. Well, she was in for a fight all right.

Four

As the receptionist showed Erin into the office, Janet Morin rose from the seat behind her desk and extended a hand.

"Erin, lovely to see you. How's Riley doing?"

"Great, thanks. Growing like a weed," Erin said and smiled in response. "And Amy? How is she?"

"The same." Janet laughed. "Sometimes I regret that I made the decision to come back to work so soon, but I know staying home with her full-time would have driven me stir-crazy! Splitting the days at home versus in the office between my husband and me has been working out wonderfully. This way, we have the best of both worlds."

Janet's husband, the other half of Morin and Morin, shared child care duties. Erin envied them their sense of unity. While James had looked forward to being a father, he'd made it clear from the outset that he wouldn't be hands-on until their baby was old enough to talk. She'd wondered if he might change his position once Riley was born, but on consideration she'd rejected the thought. Older than her by fifteen years, James had been so set in his ways he'd barely coped with the change in routine caused by marriage and sharing decision-making relating to the business. When it came to his child, he probably would have done exactly as he'd said.

Janet gestured to Erin to take a seat and settled back behind her desk.

"Tell me, what brings you here? I have to admit I was a bit curious. Don't you use the Connell family lawyers?"

Erin felt her gut clench and she forced herself to relax and breathe evenly. "Yes, we do. For the lodge, anyway. But this is of a more personal nature."

She briefly outlined the situation, thankful that Janet was already aware about the circumstances relating to Riley's conception.

"The clinic is admitting liability?" Janet asked when Erin finished speaking.

"I'm not sure, but I understand they've been closed down." She reached into her handbag. "This is the letter I was sent."

Janet took it from her and sat back, reading it carefully. "Seems a reasonable enough request," she commented, giving Erin a piercing look.

"James is Riley's father." *He has to be,* Erin amended silently.

"Let's prove it then. If it turns out that this Party A *is* Riley's father, I imagine you will want to know ahead of time exactly where you stand, right?"

"Yes." Erin exhaled on a breath before drawing in a new one. "About payment—"

"Let's not worry about that unless it looks as if we have to go to court on any of this, okay?"

Tears sprang to Erin's eyes. "Are you sure, Janet?"

"Of course I'm sure. I know you've had it tough," Janet said empathetically. "We're friends, right? Custody issues are not my specialty, but I will do more research for you. It might take me a while to get around to it because I have a rather full few days ahead, but I'll do what I can and call you, okay?"

"Thank you so much."

"Now, let's make sure we have all our details right," Janet said, reaching for a pen and paper and starting to make notes.

Erin answered Janet's questions as best she could even though the prospect of having to share custody with Riley terrified her. Rationally, she knew that if James wasn't her baby's father that Riley's biological father should have some right to his son's life. But emotionally…well, that was another story.

As a girl who'd grown up with nothing and who'd run away from home at sixteen to escape a mother who wished she'd never been born, Erin had fought hard to be where she was now—to have what she had now. And she'd gone through hell and back to have her baby boy. He was hers—heart and soul—and she'd do whatever she had to do to keep it that way.

An hour later, Erin slid her sunglasses on her face as she exited the building. She wished it were as easy to walk away from the glaring fear that held her stomach in a tight knot as it was to walk away from the building. At least she knew that Janet was taking steps to protect her and her son.

While Janet had agreed that her request for more information from the other party's lawyers was a way of
stalling things, she felt it might carry more weight if the
request came from her, acting as Erin's lawyer. She'd
also recommended that Erin instigate her own testing
to prove James was Riley's father.

This, of course, engendered its own problems. Janet
had called an independent laboratory that would courier a testing kit to Erin overnight. All she apparently
needed was a strand of James's hair, or even an old
toothbrush of his, together with a mouth swab from
Riley. That would allow the lab to extract enough DNA
to prove paternity.

Swabbing Riley's mouth would be the easy part, but
finding something of James's, that was another story.
He'd made it clear when he knew he was dying that he
didn't want her to hang on to his things unnecessarily.
Respecting his wishes, after he'd passed she'd donated
his clothes to a shelter and distributed specific possessions to his friends as he'd requested. His more personal
effects had been boxed up to give to Riley when he was
old enough to start asking about his dad. But even if
she got them out now, she doubted she'd find anything
among his photo albums and awards from which DNA
could be extracted.

She thought for a moment of the silver-backed clothes
brush that she'd also packed away. A family heirloom
that dated back to his great-grandfather, the original
Connell of Connell Lodge, she'd carefully wrapped it in
acid-free tissue and put it in the box with James's other
things. She couldn't remember ever seeing James use
the brush, but maybe there would be a stray hair still
locked within its bristles.

Satisfied she had a starting point, Erin walked toward the café where Sam had said he'd wait for her. She cast a quick look at her watch and groaned inwardly at the time. He had been waiting quite a while. Hopefully he was a patient man, although somehow that particular description wasn't the first thing that came to mind when she thought of him.

And she did think of him. A lot. Her guest had worked his way into her thoughts with next to no effort on his part. Into her thoughts and into her dreams at night. It was unsettling. She was still so newly a widow. She shouldn't be having feelings for another man like she was. But as hard as she fought against the attraction, there was a part of her that relished every moment with him. Awake or asleep.

In the dark of night she'd tried to rationalize everything. She'd gone a long time without intimacy, so it was only natural that she'd miss it. Sam was the first man she'd spent any significant time with since James's death. And even when James was alive, before he got sick, their relationship had not been sensual or physically satisfying for a while.

She and James had begun to grow apart long before they'd won the lottery run by the IVF clinic that gave them the chance to finally have a child. Trying to conceive had turned the focus of their marriage into a constant round of temperature charts and cycles and performance on command.

It was no wonder, really, that two years ago James had sought comfort in another woman's arms. When, almost a whole year later, Erin had discovered his infidelity, he'd lain the blame firmly at her feet. According to him, she'd destroyed every last moment of spontaneity in their marriage with her obsessive quest to become a mother. Of course he'd sought a simple, uncomplicated affair with someone who only craved his company and made no other demands upon him.

His words had cut deep. Erin had always believed they'd wanted the same things. A marriage that was a true partnership—sharing the day-to-day running of the business as well as their hopes and dreams for the future. Dreams that included creating a stable and loving home and a family, together. It hurt to learn that his plans were so different from hers and that he'd broken his marriage vows so easily, but she had accepted that. She had even accepted that some of the blame had lain with her for focusing all her energies into creating a child with him—that very focus, unbeknownst to her, undermining his sense of power and masculinity. But she could never entirely forgive him for his betrayal of her trust.

James had ended his affair after she'd confronted him, and then, in one of those weird twists of fate, they'd won the IVF lottery. He had said it would help solidify their marriage once the pressure of Erin becoming pregnant was off them both. She'd wanted to believe him, even though the pain of his infidelity had stuck like a splinter in the back of her mind. Of course, they hadn't counted on the bacterial infection that had attacked James's heart. He'd gone from a vital and exuberant man to a dependant and demanding shell of his former self. Their marriage had never really stood a chance to rebuild.

Erin gave herself a swift mental shake. Thinking about the past was no way to justify her reactions to Sam. He was a paying guest. That was all. She just needed a sharp reminder to keep it that way. She, better than most people, knew how life could turn on a dime.

How feelings and emotions could lead a person into difficult, and sometimes terrible, situations.

As she neared the café she saw Sam seated at one of the outdoor tables. He looked up and directly at her, then raised one arm and waved. She waved back automatically, wondering just how long she'd been standing here wool-gathering. She walked briskly toward him. As she grew nearer, she saw that his table held an empty plate, a crumpled takeout cup and a newspaper that was folded open before him. Turned to the business section, Erin noted as she drew closer.

"Sorry I took so long," she said. "Would you like to head back to the lodge?"

He flung her a smile that made the knot in her stomach tighten a little more, but this time for an entirely different reason. So much for her resolution of just a few minutes ago.

"I promised you coffee first," he said, rising from his seat. "Although, if you're in a hurry to get back to Riley…"

"No, it's okay. I nursed him not long before we left and I also left a bottle with Sasha, just in case. He'll be fine."

"What would you like?"

"A cappuccino would be great, thanks."

He was back a few moments later, setting the coffee on the table in front of her.

"Thanks," she said, lifting the takeout cup to her lips and taking a sip.

"I didn't know whether you wanted chocolate or cinnamon on top, so I told them to go for both. Is that okay?"

"More than okay. It's what I usually do," she said with a smile. "Saves making a decision that way."

Sam stiffened, his face suddenly pale.

"Are you okay?" Erin asked, concerned at the rapid change in him. "Did I say something wrong?"

"No, of course not. You just reminded me of someone for a minute."

He rubbed at his right hip and upper thigh. It was a subconscious action, Erin was sure, but she'd noticed him do that every now and then and his limp would always be more pronounced afterward.

"You're sore, aren't you? Don't bother denying it," she said with a smile. "We can head off now if you like, I can take my coffee with me."

"Are you sure you don't mind?"

"Hey, it's no problem. I did what I came here to do."

Was it her imagination or did his expression harden again? Surely she was imagining things. Sam bent to pick up a large plastic shopping bag, emblazoned with the office supply store's logo.

"You got what you wanted then?" Erin asked as they walked to the car.

"Yes. It's not high tech but it'll do the job."

He stiffened as they stopped by the car, drawing in a deep breath as if he was steeling himself for the ride back.

"Is my driving really that bad?" Erin half joked as they got in the car and Sam secured his seat belt. This time without incident.

"Don't worry about me," Sam said. "I'm just not a good passenger."

"Bad experience?" Erin probed.

"Car wreck. I'd rather not talk about it," he replied, his voice a little harsh. "Can we get going?"

"Sure," she said, clipping her seat belt safely and starting up the car.

It must have been some wreck, she thought as she negotiated her way out of the city and onto the road leading them back to the lake.

When they arrived back at the lodge Sam excused himself to head upstairs immediately, asking for his lunch on a tray, if possible. Erin was only too happy to oblige. He'd become distant and reserved—nothing like the man she'd come to know during the past few days.

Erin knew they had a spark of something between them. She couldn't possibly have imagined it. Maybe he was just one of those moody types whose disposition swung back and forth like a weather vane in a storm. She gave a mental shrug, telling herself it didn't matter at all, even while her heart gave a little twang of denial. Sam Thornton wasn't her problem; she had far more pressing matters on her mind than worrying about him.

She went through to her private rooms. After the emotional strain of telling Janet the whole story, she needed the comfort of her son.

"How did it go?" Sasha asked the instant she saw Erin.

"Okay, I guess." She looked around for Riley. "Is he down for a nap?"

"Yeah, but I don't think he'll be asleep for long. I had to give him that extra bottle you left. He's a hungry wee beast, isn't he?"

"Growth spurt, I expect," Erin answered. "I'd hoped to delay it, but I think I'm going to have to start him on solids soon."

"You think putting him on solids is bad, just wait until you have to let him go to school." Sasha patted Erin's hand, clearly understanding her reluctance to embrace this next stage of Riley's development. "Now, give me the details. What did the lawyer say?"

Erin skirted over the basics of the discussion she'd had. "She's going to do more research for me but feels it's important to first establish that James was Riley's father. So now I have to find something with a trace of James's DNA on it."

"It's all very *CSI,* isn't it?" Sasha said, her forehead wrinkling into a frown of concentration. "You gave most of his stuff away, didn't you?"

"Yeah, although I did keep the important things for Riley for when he's old enough to understand. There's an old coat brush in amongst those things that might hold a hair. Aside from that I have no idea how I'm going to find anything."

Sasha reached across and gave Erin's shoulder a squeeze. "You'll come up with something. Probably where you least expect it. Have a little faith. I'd better go. Call me when you find what you're looking for, okay?"

Thinking she needed more than a *little* faith Erin saw her friend out, thanking her for caring for Riley.

"It's no problem," Sasha insisted. "You know I love spending time with your little guy."

After Sasha had gone Erin put a quick lunch on a tray for Sam and took it upstairs. She knocked gently on the door to the room she'd given him as an office and went inside. He was staring intently at his laptop screen.

"Lunch," she said quietly. "Where would you like me to put it?"

Sam gestured to a clear patch at the edge of the desk, without so much as lifting his gaze from the computer. Erin did as he bade and turned to leave him to his own devices. She was on the verge of closing the door behind her when his voice stopped her in her tracks.

"Erin, can you come back a moment?"

She turned and came back into the room. "Is there a problem?"

"Yeah," he said, his cool gray eyes lifting to meet hers. "I'm sorry I was short with you. It was rude of me."

"No problem," she hastened to reassure him. After all, he hadn't come here for her company, had he? Even so, his apology soothed a bit of the sting of his earlier abruptness.

"It *is* a problem. I'm not usually so impolite. Something you said reminded me of someone. It upset me and I let that affect my manners."

"Something *I* said?" Erin repeated, confused.

"At the coffee shop, you said something my wife used to say. My *late* wife."

"Oh," she breathed on a sigh of understanding. "I'm sorry."

"No," he said, rising from his seat. "I'm the one who's sorry. I shouldn't have reacted that way. If it's okay with you, could I still eat dinner with you in the kitchen tonight? I...I'd rather not eat alone."

Compassion flooded her. She'd been lucky to have Riley to keep her thoughts occupied at mealtimes but she well knew, and understood, the loneliness that came after the loss of a spouse, especially in the everyday things that you'd always taken for granted. She managed a tremulous smile. "Sure, that's no problem. Dinner at six, then?"

Sam nodded. "Thanks, that'll be great."

An awkward silence opened between them. Erin looked at the printer now installed on the desk. "You got the printer hooked up okay?"

"Yeah, it's all doing what it's supposed to."

"Good. I'll see you downstairs at dinner, then."

Erin left the room feeling a little better than she'd felt earlier. Sam's sudden shift in temperament was now explained, which left her with only one more problem. Where the heck was she going to find something with James's DNA?

Five

Sam heard the door close quietly behind him and bracketed his head with his hands. This entire exercise was proving harder than he'd anticipated. He'd thought it would be simple. Come to Tahoe, stay at Connell Lodge.

See his son.

He hadn't expected for a moment to feel drawn to the baby's mother, nor had he expected her to remind him so viscerally of his late wife. It wasn't so much in a physical sense—the two women looked nothing alike. Laura's porcelain skin and dark red hair had been nothing like the glow of summer-kissed skin and short black hair that Erin sported so effortlessly. But it was in their natures, their nurturing instincts—no matter who walked within their spheres. And it attracted and repelled him at the same time.

After Laura's death, Sam had sworn not to love another woman again. Not only did he not deserve to, he couldn't trust himself. Everything in his life he'd done to the very best of his abilities, and he'd set the bar high. Yet with his wife, he'd failed. Failed on the most basic level. And that failure had cost her life. As he'd lain in a hospital bed in the aftermath of their car smash he'd welcomed the pain of his injuries, and afterward, the agony of rehabilitation and learning to walk again. Every torturous step was a just punishment for what he'd done.

His life had become defined by his guilt and his failure. Even the company he'd created from a speck of an idea and grown into a multinational software empire failed to hold his interest any longer. He'd dwelled within a dark place for the past year and a bit. A dark place lit only recently by the information that Riley Connell may be his son. Suddenly he had something to strive for, someone to live for again. Someone to build a world around.

Even now, just thinking about the boy made his heart squeeze. Already he could see a family likeness. The baby had the Thornton nose and the stubborn set to Riley's chin was so like Sam's own and his father's before him. Was he tilting at windmills? Seeing things he wanted to see? He wouldn't know for certain until Erin consented to stop delaying the DNA testing.

He huffed a deprecating laugh. They'd gone beyond consent the minute he'd seen her walk into that lawyer's office today. David would rustle up that court order, using whatever favors he could pull and Erin would *have* to agree. Sam didn't want to wait any longer. He wanted to know now. He needed to be a part of Riley's life, his future.

Sam pushed his chair away from the desk and strode

over to the window, staring out at the lake. It was beautiful here. An amazing place for a child to grow up. How would Riley cope, he wondered, sharing his time between the edge of the lake and Sam's inner-city apartment? It would be all very well while he was small, but Sam wanted his son to attend the best schools, to have advantages geared toward his future that he wouldn't have here. Would Erin agree?

He shoved a hand through his hair. He was jumping the gun a bit. A bit? he asked himself ruefully. A whole freaking lot. Everything hinged on those tests. Everything.

His very world.

By the time he headed downstairs later that day, he'd pushed his mood behind him. As he approached the kitchen, he could hear Riley's fractious griping followed by Erin's soothing tones and he felt a new appreciation for her. She'd been raising Riley single-handedly. It was no easy task and yet he hadn't heard a single word of complaint from her about it. Erin was stirring something on the stove as he entered and Riley gave a squeal of recognition as Sam entered the room.

"Oh, it's you. I'm sorry, but dinner's running a bit late tonight," Erin said over her shoulder.

She sounded tired and distracted.

"No problem. That lunch kept me going and it's not as if I've been burning off energy," Sam said, lowering himself to the table and handing Riley the toy he'd flung to the tabletop.

"Do you want to go into the main sitting room, watch a bit of TV maybe?" Erin suggested.

Was she trying to get rid of him? "No, I'm fine. Is there anything I can do to help?"

"Sam, you're a guest here. You're not supposed to help."

"It's not like you're overrun with staff." He smiled in return. "And I don't mind chipping in when I can."

Riley threw his toy down again and instantaneously began to fuss. Sam picked up the toy again and handed it back to Riley, wondering just how long this game had been going on. Quite a while, if the tense set of Erin's shoulders and her pale face were anything to go by.

"Look, I'm sorry," Erin said putting down her spoon and wiping her hands on a towel tucked into the waist-band of her jeans. "He's not normally this demanding. He slept a bit too long while we were away and then wouldn't settle for his afternoon nap, so he's overtired and grumpy."

Sam chuckled. "I know how he feels. Can I take him for a walk outside for a bit? Would that help?"

He saw the relief on her face rapidly chased away by guilt. "I couldn't ask you to do that."

"Hey," he said softly. "I offered."

He could see the battle on Erin's expressive features and knew he'd won when she sighed and said, "I'll get his stroller and his blanket, then."

Outside, the evening air had a slight chill to it, a re-minder that summer was on its way out and that fall wasn't far away. The bay was still and settled with the dark shadows of the tall trees on the perimeter begin-ning to cast long shadows across the surface. Sam hun-kered down beside the stroller and pointed to a pair of birds flying by, but Riley's attention was already cap-tured by them.

Sam took the opportunity to study the baby's face in more detail. No, he hadn't been mistaken. Riley's chin hinted at the same square line of his own, of the same dimple that was a trait of all the Thornton men. Riley had to be his, he just knew it, *felt it*—and when the little boy turned his face back to Sam and gave him a gummy smile, Sam felt his heart squeeze tight.

"He's settled down then," Erin commented from behind him.

Sam straightened to his feet. She looked more relaxed now. More like the capable woman he'd seen from the day he'd arrived.

"Yeah, maybe he just needed a change of scenery."

"You're good with him. Do you have kids of your own?" Erin asked.

Sam swallowed against the lump that formed in his throat. "My wife and I had hoped for a family. She died before we could start one."

And here it would come, he thought, mentally bracing himself. The same platitudes that his family and friends had cast at him with the best of intentions. He could still meet someone new, start again, have a family. But he couldn't. It would be a betrayal of Laura's memory. But Erin surprised him in even this.

"It must be hard," she said simply.

"Some times are worse than others, but I'm getting there."

"As we do." Erin sighed and looked out over the lake.

Sam followed her gaze, saw it settle on the large launch moored at the end of the pier.

"Yours?" he asked.

Erin nodded. "It's part of the lodge. Fishing charters used to be part of the appeal of staying here. We stopped them when Riley's dad got sick."

Sam fought back the bitter taste that flooded his mouth every time he heard the other man referred to as Riley's father. He wanted to point to his own chest and say firmly, "It's *me*. I'm Riley's father." But he didn't have the right. Yet.

"Are you going to start them up again, the charters?" he forced himself to say before he said something else he might regret.

"I don't have a license. James did all that. I've thought about selling the launch, but I think I'd be better off to simply hire someone to take charters for the lodge again. I know it would increase our guest traffic. It's on the list of things to do—the very long list." She sighed. "Well, dinner's ready. Are you coming inside?"

Sam wished he could hold on to the moment here a little longer, but he knew the temperature would drop rapidly once the sun was gone. "Sure."

Erin took control of the stroller and wheeled Riley back toward the house. Sam followed slowly in their wake.

She was just doing her rounds, checking the downstairs of the house to ensure that everything was all locked and secure for the night, when she noticed the library light was still on. Erin popped her head around the door and smiled at Sam, who was seated in a deep leather button-back chair by the fireside, a book open in his lap, but his attention fixed on the flames cavorting merrily over the logs in the fireplace. She'd lit the fire after they'd finished their meal as a sudden chill had invaded the air. The flames' cheerful brightness was a strong contrast to the solemn set of his face.

"Everything okay?" she asked. "I'm about to turn in, but can I get you anything before I go?"

"Sit with me for a while, Erin. It's still early."

Erin was torn. Despite his apology, she still felt the caustic sting of his curtness earlier today. It made her wary. Besides, she had enough on her plate right now and certainly didn't want to make things even more complicated by falling in love or anything silly like that.

Falling in love? What on earth was she thinking? She was still newly widowed. Granted, her marriage had been strained for some years before James had died, the love wrung out of it rather than strengthened by their attempts to have a family, but she still owed something to James's memory. He hadn't been the perfect husband she'd fantasized about when she'd planned her future as a teenager, but he'd still given her so much. All she'd ever wanted was a real home and a family, and thanks to James she had a beautiful house and a perfect son. She'd always be grateful to him for both. Sam had given her nothing but heated surges of attraction that reminded her how long it had been since she'd really felt like a beautiful, desirable woman....

She gave herself a mental shake. No, she couldn't justify her crazy reaction to a handsome man. Especially one she'd known little more than a few days. She was better than that. Stronger than that.

If only to prove to herself that she could overcome this...this ridiculous hormonal allure, she found herself seated opposite Sam.

"Good book?" she asked in the silence that suddenly opened between them.

He flicked a look at the tome on his lap, almost appearing surprised to find it there. He laughed, the sound making her gut clench. He didn't laugh nearly enough and the sound of it warmed her to her core.

"To be honest I couldn't tell you if it's good or not. I grabbed it off the shelf and opened it and that was about all."

Erin laughed with him. It felt good to be relaxed in his company.

"Not a huge amount of popular fiction in here," Erin commented, letting her eyes slide over the many hard-back and leather-bound covers. "How's your own book coming along?"

"Slowly. It's more of a manual, really. My firm designs and develops software."

"Sounds exciting," she said drily.

"It's definitely not, which is why I'm in here rather than back upstairs where I should be working." He sighed deeply. "I would normally have done this at home, but there are too many reminders."

"Your wife?"

"Yeah, Laura."

"Pretty name."

"Pretty woman. She would've given anything to be a mother, like you." He raised a hand and rubbed his eyes. "I blame myself for her death. It's not something I find easy to live with."

Erin stiffened in her chair, her breath frozen in her chest. "Surely you're not respons—"

"I was driving the car when we were broadsided—it was my fault. I ran a red light because we were late for an appointment. No, *I* was late, so I tried to make up time." His voice was bitter and angry.

Erin didn't know what to say in the silence that stretched out between them. What could anyone say when the facts were stated so baldly? She jumped as a log of wood suddenly snapped, sending a shoot of sparks up the chimney.

"I'm sorry," Sam said, carefully placing his book on a side table and getting up to stand by the fire. "I shouldn't be off-loading to you."

"It's okay," Erin said.

"No, it's not. I have tried to deal with it, to come to terms with what I did, the choices I made that day. I still can't believe I was so stupid, so bloody reckless and arrogant." His hands balled into fists at his sides.

"Are you succeeding in dealing with it?" she asked softly.

She could see the muscles in Sam's jaw clench tight for a moment before he spoke.

"Most of the time. She just deserved so much more, y'know? I put my business first for most of our marriage. I certainly did so that day. If I'd just delegated one small thing, and left the office on time, she'd still be alive today."

Erin rose to stand beside him, placing one hand on his forearm. Beneath her touch she felt his muscles were tense—his rage against himself a palpable thing.

"You can't say that. Anything else could have delayed you that day. Any number of things could have come up."

Sam gave her a twisted smile. "You're a fatalist then?"

She shook her head. "I just think that some things simply happen. Questioning them after the event is futile. We can't turn back time, no matter how much we want to."

"And the future? Do you think we can change what's going to happen there?"

There was a note of desperation in his voice that pulled at her every instinct to comfort, to offer solace from whatever demons rode him.

"I don't know," she said after a small hesitation. "I'd like to think we learn from our mistakes, something at least."

"Yeah," he said brokenly. "Me, too."

He still sounded so lost and unhappy, as if, even though he'd said the words, he didn't really believe they were true. Erin didn't stop to think. She lifted her face to his, her lips slightly parted, and kissed him.

His body jerked, as if he'd received an electric shock, but almost instantly she felt him begin to relax. He angled his head slightly, the better to return her kiss, she realized, and his hands slid around her waist to her lower back, pulling her into him. She went willingly, not allowing herself to think about how wrong this was. All she could think about was how right he felt and, when he opened his mouth to deepen their kiss, how right he tasted.

Her body, so long dormant—attuned only to her most basic needs of survival and to those of her infant son— began a slow burn. Her hands slid up Sam's arms, feeling the muscles that were so taut with anger a moment ago, loosen and soften under her touch.

When he pulled her hard against him, she felt a jolt of pure sexual hunger spear through her, and she knew he felt the same way. The hardened ridge of his arousal pressed against her mound and she let her instincts override the last bastion of good sense as she flexed against him.

Her entire body roared to life with need for him, for his touch, for the heavy male weight of him. When he shoved his hands under her T-shirt, she quivered with delight as his long fingers stroked her skin. She arched her back, pressing her hips against him once more. Sam's lips left her mouth, tracing a new path along her jaw and the cord of her neck. She shivered again as she felt the slightly rough rasp of his unshaven cheeks on her skin, and welcomed the feel of it.

He made her feel vital, female, desirable. When his lips traveled back up her throat and recaptured her mouth she moaned, parting her lips to give him free access to the soft, moist depths. His tongue gently swept her lips before probing deeper.

And then, suddenly, awfully, it was all over. Sam's hands pulled hers from behind his neck and dragged them down. His breathing labored in his chest, his eyes glittered like rain-washed slate. He let her go and took a step away. She wanted to protest, to reach for him again. To relive what they'd just shared, but it was all she could do to stand on her own two feet without collapsing.

"We shouldn't—" he started.

"No! Don't! Don't say we shouldn't have done that," she said as firmly as she could. Summoning every last ounce of strength she possessed, she smiled at him and said, "It was right, for us, at the time. Let's leave it there, shall we?"

She couldn't bear to hear his denial. To have him reduce what they'd just shared to a mistake. She turned and forced her legs to move, to take her away from him and from the temptation he offered.

So much for proving herself better than her hormones.

Six

Erin was a jangle of nerves by the time she reached her rooms. She paced the floor of her living room, back and forth, almost wearing a hole in the carpet before she made herself sit down and take stock of what had happened.

She'd never been so forward before in her life and her behavior both shocked and thrilled her. Even thinking about it now, she didn't regret for a minute what she'd done. But did Sam?

She hadn't wanted to hear him say they shouldn't have done what they did, but the words still echoed silently in her head. Maybe it was wrong. Maybe she had taken advantage of him, his grief. Now there was a turn around from the typical, she thought. Wasn't it supposed to be men who took advantage in that way?

She shook her head at herself. She was so wound up now she'd never get any rest, at least not unless she found some way to rid herself of the tension that held her in its grip. Maybe a deep, relaxing soak would help. Erin drove herself to her feet. She'd check on Riley and then draw herself a bath. She was almost sorry to see he was still sound asleep in his crib—his little fists flung wide on either side of his head. Her heart clamped hard on the surge of love that swelled within her. She loved him so very much. Would lay down her life for him, without question.

How could any mother not feel the same way about their child, she wondered. This fierce protective instinct was as natural to her as breathing. Not for the first time, Erin wondered why her own mother had not been prepared to love and protect Erin the way Erin was prepared to love and protect Riley. The old familiar pain of rejection plucked at her, tearing away her hard-won confidence and belief in herself.

Had she really been so very unlovable that her own mother had screamed at her, over and over, that she'd wished Erin had never been born? Erin bit hard on her lip to stop the sharp cry that built in her throat. She closed her eyes and dragged an uneven breath into her tortured chest.

Even her own husband hadn't loved her as she'd yearned to be loved. They'd slid into marriage because it was convenient, not out of any burning passion for each other. Was that it? Had she craved the wildness of passion? The sheer indulgence of giving in to want and need, and to hell with the consequences? Was that why she'd taken the opportunity to kiss Sam Thornton tonight? A man she barely knew? A paying guest under her roof?

From the moment she'd first seen him she'd been aware of a visceral consciousness of him on every level.

He made her feel alive again. It was an intoxicating sensation, frightening and exhilarating at the same time. She was attracted to him on so many levels she almost felt dizzy with it. Kissing him had been crazy—wild. And she wanted to do it again. Kiss, and everything that came next. Did that make her a bad person? She had no answers.

Erin let herself out of Riley's room before her uneasy presence disturbed his sleep and went through to her bathroom. She twisted the old faucets open over the deep tub and let the water run; a cloud of steam soon filled the air. Somewhere in the vanity unit she had some relaxing bath crystals. They'd been a farewell gift from a guest a few years ago and she'd shoved them in there, meaning to use them one day. Well, if she ever needed relaxing, now was the time.

She shoved aside some old bathroom supplies. She really needed to clean out in here one of these days. Another job to add to the bottom of her ever-increasing list of things to do, she thought with a sigh.

A black case fell with a clatter to the shelf below, knocking over a collection of old bottles of lotion and sunscreen. Erin lifted the case, ready to shove it back where it came from, but her hand stilled as she touched it.

James's toiletries bag. The one she'd brought home from the hospital the night he'd passed away. What on earth had she been thinking, putting it back in here? She pulled the small black leather case out of the cupboard and yanked the zipper open, exposing the contents. Her heart almost shuddered to a halt in her chest. A toothbrush. More important, James's toothbrush. Finally, she had something with his DNA. A way of proving, once and for all, that *he,* and not some stranger, was Riley's father.

Erin stood, put the case on top of the vanity and quickly turned off the taps before going into the kitchen to find a zip-seal plastic bag to hold the toothbrush. When that courier pack arrived tomorrow she wanted to be sure she could send it straight back out again. Then all her immediate worries would be solved.

The next morning, as Sam made his way downstairs to the kitchen, he felt like a bear with a sore head. Last night had been madness. A delicious madness that had left him feeling frustrated and torn and racked with guilt. Kissing Erin Connell had been yet another betrayal to rack up on his list of failures to his dead wife. And yet, if it had been so wrong, why had Erin felt so very right in his arms? Why had the taste of her been so enthralling, so addictive? Why had he wanted more?

Pushing her away from him had been one of the hardest things he'd had to do in over a year. He'd wanted her with a need that went so deep he wondered how he'd be able to continue to stay here and still keep his distance. Yet the prospect of leaving was even more abhorrent to him.

Her parting words rang in his mind, over and over. *"It was right, for us, at the time."* At the time. And what about the next time? And the time after that? Would he be capable of saying no? Did he even want to? Sam resolutely pushed the unanswered questions to the back of his mind, but they kept shoving right back to the fore.

It was time to be honest. He wanted Erin Connell. Wanted her in the way a man wants a woman. The first question was, did she want him just as much? If her response to him was any indicator she certainly did. But

even more important, could he bear to live with himself
if he followed up on the mixed feelings that clouded his
every waking thought?

When he got to the kitchen he hesitated in the doorway. The room was empty, the benches cleared. A note
sat on the worn kitchen table.

*Good morning, Sam, I set your breakfast choices out
in the main dining room. –Erin.*

The main dining room? The giant room that, although very tastefully appointed, was best suited to
a gathering of ten to twenty people? She was avoiding him, obviously. Maybe their kiss had rattled her
more than she'd wanted to admit to his face. He smiled
grimly. Well, he'd see about that. Sam limped to the dining room, where chafing dishes were set up on the old-
fashioned sideboard. He heaped a plate with scrambled
eggs, hash browns and strips of bacon, poured himself a
generous mug full of steaming fresh coffee, and just as
determinedly limped back to what he'd begun to think
of as *his* seat at the kitchen table.

He was just finishing his coffee when Erin came
through from her private rooms, sealing a large courier
pack she was carrying. She started when she saw him
at the table, almost dropping the package.

"Oh, you surprised me," she said, tightening her grip
on the packet and turning the address to face her. "Is
there a problem in the dining room?"

Sam shook his head. "Not at all. I just prefer to eat
here." He hesitated and gave her a steady look. "Unless
you have any objections, that is?"

"No," she said cautiously. "I don't mind. I just
thought you'd prefer a bit of distance, after…"

He caught her hand and held it in his own. Her fingers were long and delicate, her nails short and practi-

cal, but he remembered full well how that hand had felt pressed against him, how those nails had bitten through the fine cotton of his shirt and into his skin, the sensations her touch had sent coursing through his body.

"After our kiss?" he said gently. "Don't worry. You were right about it being what was right for us, right then. I think we've both been through the wringer and we both deserve a bit of comfort. Thank you."

He let her hand go and saw the way she curled her fingers tight before flicking them out loosely again. Did her skin tingle the same way his did? Had a shot of something intense and instinctive rocketed through her as it had him? Even now he was semi-aroused just looking at her. Her breathing was rapid, her chest rising and falling in a way that was almost mesmerizing. Her soft full lips fell open, as if she was on the verge of saying something but had forgotten already what it was she wanted to say.

"Right," she said awkwardly, before nodding to herself. "I'll be out for the morning. Do you have everything you need?"

Sam's gaze remained fixed on her lips for several full seconds before he raised it to meet her eyes. "For now," he said. "Thanks."

He rose from his seat and took his plates to the sink.

"Oh, don't. Seriously, you don't need to do that," Erin protested.

"I'm quite capable of rinsing a couple of dishes."

"Well, if you're sure you don't mind," she said, catching her lower lip between her teeth.

"Hey, if I minded I wouldn't be doing it, okay?"

She gave that little nod again. "I'm heading into town with Riley but I'll be back by lunchtime."

"Whatever. I can see to myself if you're not back on time."

"But—"

She looked as if she was about to protest again but Sam raised a hand. "One of your promises on your website is that you create a home away from home here at Connell Lodge. At home, I pretty much look after myself so I'm comfortable doing the same here, within limits," he finished with a smile.

"All right, I believe you." She smiled in return, but he noticed it didn't quite reach her eyes.

Erin started to leave the room but he called her name, stopping her in her tracks. When she turned to face him he raised a hand to her face, touching her cheek ever so softly with the knuckle of his index finger.

"Take care on the road, okay?"

"I will," she murmured. "I definitely will."

It had been a week since their kiss. A week loaded with confusing yet exhilarating thoughts and feelings. Seven days punctuated with accidental touches and, Erin suspected, some not-so-accidental touches that had left her nerves strung deliciously taut in a way she'd never experienced before.

They hadn't kissed again, and Erin found herself reliving that encounter at odd moments of the day. Reliving it and wanting to repeat it.

Even the other night, when they'd both been on the floor in the library with Riley lying between them. The lights had been low and the fire blazing from behind a protective screen—creating an ambiance that had locked the three of them together in a contented cocoon. They'd been laughing indulgently together when they'd realized Riley had drifted off to sleep, and their eyes had met. Anticipation had thrilled through her as their gazes locked, as Sam had leaned forward just that much that she'd instinctively copied his motion until their bodies had formed an arch over the slumbering child between them. She'd parted her lips ever so slightly, watched as his eyes had dropped to her mouth. Her heartbeat had kicked up a notch. But then Sam had pulled away and made some excuse about attending to work.

His rather rapid departure had done nothing to cool her blood or what she openly acknowledged now as a fast-growing desire for him. A desire that ensured Sam Thornton occupied the better part of her waking thoughts—and her sleeping ones, if truth be told. She felt as giddy as a teenager embarking on a first love.

And was it her first love? She'd spent a lot of time soul-searching in the quieter moments of the past few days, asking herself over and over again if that was true. The painful facts had been a sobering realization. One that made her not like herself terribly much.

She knew she hadn't loved James the way she ought to have. In retrospect, she could see how he'd appealed to her. He was older, very stable, very sure of himself in his world. His interest in her had grown during the time she'd worked here, after she'd escaped from the mess she'd made of her life in Sacramento. By the time he'd asked her to marry him she'd convinced herself she must love him. In reality, she'd loved what he represented more. She'd clung to his interest in her—to his offer of marriage and a respectable, stable, secure life—with both hands and held on fast.

So fast, she'd eventually strangled the life out of any chance of a true marriage together. Fixated on creating the perfect home, the perfect marriage, the perfect family, Erin had eventually driven away the man who could have made that all possible. Driven him straight into the arms of a woman who had offered him the kind of uncomplicated and loving relationship he'd had every right to expect from his wife.

Erin had one chance now, to make good to James the promise she'd made as he'd struggled for his final breaths—that she'd bring Riley up here at Connell Lodge. That she'd infuse in him the love for the place his father had always had and his forefathers before him.

The special delivery envelope that had arrived this morning burned in the back pocket of her jeans where she'd shoved it, unwilling to open the missive until she knew she'd be on her own with no chance of being interrupted. Sam was locked upstairs in his office, Riley was down for a nap.

Erin poured herself a mug of coffee from the carafe she constantly refreshed during the day and took the letter outside to the lawn furniture. It wouldn't be long now before she'd have to put everything in storage for the coming cooler months. She also made a mental note to look into dry-stack storage for the launch. Another expense she wasn't looking forward to.

She tugged the envelope that'd been sent from the laboratory from her pocket, and set it on the table in front of her before sitting down in a chair. A light breeze tickled the back of her neck.

Taking a deep breath, Erin smoothed out the envelope and slid the tip of her finger under the seal. She pulled out the lab report, reading each word carefully, barely understanding the scientific jargon. But one thing she did understand, and her hand was shaking as she

neatly refolded the results and slid them back into the
envelope.

James Connell was not Riley's father.

Seven

Erin rose on unsteady legs to go back inside. She grabbed the cordless phone from its stand in the kitchen, shut herself in her bedroom and dialed Morin and Morin's number.

"Erin, I'm glad you called. I was going to call you today. How are you?" Janet's warm and friendly voice filled her ear.

"Not so good," Erin admitted.

"You have your results?" Janet's voice was all business.

"I do, and…" She choked back a sob. "And they're not good. James wasn't Riley's father."

"I see," Janet said after a short silence. "Well, that brings me to what I needed to talk to you about. I've received a court order requesting that you and Riley provide DNA samples per Party A's request to establish paternity."

"I can't fight it now, can I?" Erin's voice shook.

"Not with the court order. Plus the swabs will need to be done under supervision with legal representatives there from both sides. I can suggest they be done here at my office if that would make you more comfortable."

Nothing right now would make her comfortable. Erin shook her head in mute denial, even though she knew she'd have to comply. She swallowed against the lump in her throat. "When?"

"In the next few days would be best. How about I work things out with the other lawyers and get back to you, hmm? Any time in particular that's not suitable?"

"The rest of forever?" Erin suggested brokenly.

Janet didn't laugh. "I'm sorry, Erin. But we have to do it. If this guy is Riley's dad he has rights—you can't deny him those. Nor can you deny Riley's rights to know his real father."

"I know," Erin said softly on a sigh.

She ended the call asking Janet to let her know when the meeting was arranged then sat, numb, on the bed. How could James not be Riley's father? It was the final, cruelest blow in a series of them. How could such a mistake have been made? She wrapped her arms around her stomach and rocked gently on the bed, fighting back the urge to let go of her fear and scream out loud.

She had to somehow keep this all in, keep it to herself, at least until the results of the next test came through. She started to grab at straws as her mind scattered on a myriad of possibilities. Maybe this Party A wasn't Riley's father either. Maybe some other man was, some stranger who had no wish to establish paternity and turn their lives completely upside down. Not to mention turn them both out of their home. If the clinic had made a mistake between two families, surely the mistake could easily extend beyond that?

Hard on that thought came another. What if James's sperm had been used to fertilize another couple's egg? What if he had a direct descendant somewhere out there? Someone who had a legitimate claim on Connell Lodge? A legitimate claim on her and her baby's home that she no longer had?

The snowball of terror just kept growing bigger and bigger in Erin's mind. She pushed herself up off the bed and forced herself into activity. She had to keep busy, so busy she wouldn't have time to think or time to ponder the reality she now faced. She could only hope that the next round of tests would prove Party A was not Riley's birth father. That way, she could continue the charade that James was Riley's dad and she and Riley could stay in the only true home she'd ever known. She didn't want to think about what would happen if the trustees who oversaw the Connell affairs discovered the truth.

She'd been homeless before and she'd sworn she'd never slide that low ever, ever again. Now, because of Riley, it was even more important that she hold on to the roof over her head. He didn't deserve to lose what should have been his birthright just because of some stupid mistake.

Anger slowly began to replace the fear that had threatened to consume her. Anger and determination. She would protect what they had, for Riley's sake. No matter what came her way.

Erin was still antsy later that night and Riley had picked up on her mood, testing her patience to its outer limits. It was all she could do not to cry in sympathy when she put him, protesting loudly, down for the night.

She resolutely clipped the baby monitor to her belt and gathered her cleaning supplies. He'd settle, he had to. And then she could lose herself in the rhythms of keeping Connell Lodge fit for habitation. Okay, so maybe that was a slight exaggeration. She kept the old house in excellent order, but she did miss the additional help that a full complement of staff had brought.

Before James's illness, they'd had two live-in staff as well as a roster of part-timers who came to assist with the outdoor work and the cleaning inside. Now, she just had to grab time wherever and whenever she could. It wasn't ideal, Erin thought as she went into the library and flicked her duster along the shelves, but it would have to do. At least until she could get some cash flow going again and hire a part-timer to help around the place.

She found a peaceful rhythm in the housework, in the scent of the polish she used on the wooden furniture and the leather treatment she used on the chairs. It got her thinking about the past.

When she'd found work here at the lodge she thought she'd landed in heaven. It was a long way from the run-down trailer park where she'd grown up on the outskirts of Sacramento, and even further from the abandoned building where she'd lived with a group of itinerants after years of running away from her mother's abuse.

That had ended badly. Very badly. The taste of bile rose in Erin's throat and her hand settled on the monitor at her hip, turning up the volume. Riley had settled, but just thinking about the past, about what had happened, sent her flying back down the hall to their rooms to check on him. She pushed open his bedroom door and peeked into his crib. He lay there like an angel—

his beautiful lashes spread in tiny twin fans on cheeks still flushed from his earlier crying.

Erin reached down to straighten his covers—resting her hand on his little tummy, feeling the rapid draw in and out of his breaths. He was okay. She breathed deeply, settling the old jangle of nerves that had spooked her as she'd thought of the past. Of someone else's baby who hadn't been as loved as her little boy. A baby they'd all failed. Yes, Riley was okay. She was doing everything right. This time around.

A sound in the kitchen filtered down the hallway. She gave Riley a gentle loving pat and left his room, pulling his door closed behind her. She was surprised to see Sam in the kitchen. He'd had dinner on a tray in his study tonight, saying he was finally on a roll with his book and didn't want to take a break. She fought back a smile as she took in his unusually disheveled appearance.

"Tough day?" she asked, entering the room.

"You have no idea. You'd think I knew better. That I'd have backed up."

"You didn't?"

He shoved a hand through his short-cropped hair, making it stand in all directions. "I'm an idiot. I saved over my file. All that work today, gone."

"Hey, we all make mistakes. Don't be too hard on yourself. Besides, aren't you the software guru? You must be able to retrieve something, surely?"

He barked an ironic laugh. "You'd think so, wouldn't you? But no such luck."

"Maybe you just need a break. You've been working hard all day. Why not come into my sitting room, have a coffee or something and we can just talk."

In the back of her mind, Erin thought about all the

things she still had to do this evening, but right now it seemed more important to give Sam the comfort he so obviously needed. Besides, she could do with some company herself after revisiting—however briefly—the memories of her past.

"Sure, I'd like that," Sam said.

"Coffee then?" Erin asked, moving toward the machine.

"Actually, I wouldn't mind a glass of something stronger."

"No problem. Wine or spirits?"

"I'd kill for a whiskey about now." Sam smiled.

Erin laughed. "You go and take a seat." She gestured to the doorway to her sitting room. "I'll pour your drink."

She reached up to the top shelf of the glass-fronted hutch for a cut-crystal tumbler, then took a bottle of aged single malt from the cupboard beneath and poured a generous measure. She started to walk toward the sitting room but hesitated for a moment by the wine fridge. She hadn't had an alcoholic drink since the IVF procedures had begun—even before then she'd almost completely stopped drinking alcohol. It had gotten her into enough trouble in the past, but tonight was different.

Making a decision, she put Sam's drink down and quickly poured herself a small glass of a chilled Napa Valley Pinot Gris. She'd nursed Riley before bed and she was certain he would sleep through until early morning. She'd been assured by her doctor that one glass of wine now and then would be okay, provided she didn't drink within four hours or so of nursing.

Erin took the two drinks through to her sitting room and found Sam studying a montage of baby photos on the wall that she'd accumulated of Riley—starting with his first ultrasound.

"Pretty amazing, isn't it?" she said, handing him his drink.

"Life never fails to amaze me." He took the glass and raised it to her in a small toast. "To a job well done."

"So far," she concurred, taking a small sip of her wine.

"Hey, don't be so hard on yourself. You're doing a great job with Riley. It can't be easy on your own."

"No, it's not. But it is worth every second."

"Hear, hear," he said, taking a sip of his whiskey. "Ah, that's good."

Erin gestured for him to sit down and took a seat on the couch opposite.

"Have you ever thought of marrying ag—" Sam shut himself off and took a deep breath before continuing. "Look, I'm sorry. That was insensitive of me. I hate it when people say the same to me about my future. I have no plans to ever marry again so I don't know why I thought it was all right for me to suggest you should."

"No need to apologize, Sam. It's okay. Besides, I have no plans to marry again until Riley is at least old enough to take over the lodge. It's his legacy. Handed down generation to generation of Connells. And it's my job to make sure he has something worth inheriting."

Somehow she had to continue to believe she could carry it off.

"That's quite a commitment. Putting your whole life on hold for your son? What if he doesn't want to work the lodge?"

Erin shrugged. "I'll cross that bridge when I get there. In the meantime, it's our home and our income. I'm duty bound to protect that."

"Is it what you want to do?"

"It's what I have to do. Management of the property has been handed over from father to son since the original James Connell. Riley's father was the last and Riley will be next. It's his legacy."

She said the last words emphatically, as if by saying them aloud it could make them true.

And if Riley was *his* son? Sam thought. Where would that leave Erin? No wonder she was dragging her heels about the DNA testing. This home was her son's birthright—but only if he was her husband's biological child.

Sam gave her a searching look and whistled softly. "Heck of a responsibility."

"I know, which is why I have to get it right. Build the business back up again and make sure Riley has something worth inheriting. James and I closed down operations when he became ill, let our staff go. It was a hard decision but the lodge was too much for me to run on my own while I was pregnant and then after Riley was born. And when we found out James wouldn't get better, it was too late to change our minds."

"You didn't want to put managers in, just to keep the business running?"

"No. I did suggest it, but this was James's family home as well as our business. He didn't want strangers making decisions he should be making. He was pretty old-fashioned that way."

Sam looked at Erin. She looked tired. Worn-out, really. As if all the cares of the world had settled on her shoulders. He knew the feeling, and also knew how hard it was to pull yourself out of the darkness.

A sudden yawn seemed to catch her by surprise.

"You're tired," Sam said immediately, rising from his seat. "I'm keeping you."

"No, it's okay," Erin protested. "Please, sit down. Finish your drink."

He sat down again and watched as she took another small sip of her wine, admiring her grace as she did so. Even though she always seemed as though she was on the go, she did so with a fluidity of movement that he found distinctly appealing. Since their kiss last week, he'd found himself watching her at the oddest times. He even left his office door open sometimes when she came up to make up his room or replace the linen. Seeing her bend over the bed and smooth out the comforter, watching how the fit of her jeans was so perfect across her hips and the softly rounded curves of her buttocks—it had been a slow and silent torment. One he'd begun to relish.

"Forgive me for asking," he began, leaning forward just a little in his chair. "But you seem a bit distracted tonight. Something on your mind?"

She laughed, a self-deprecating sound. "You could say that," she admitted.

"Anything I can help you with? As clichéd as it is, you know what they say—a problem shared is a problem halved."

"I think I'm beyond sharing my problems," she said with a wry twist to her mouth. "I've gotten so used to handling everything on my own. Thanks, but don't worry, I'll be fine. Riley was a bit of a handful today and I got a little behind on things is all."

"Maybe I can mind him for you occasionally during the day," Sam suggested, his heart beating a little faster. Would she go for it? She'd been a perfect hostess so far, ensuring that Riley's daily routines didn't impinge on his as a guest at the lodge, but he'd give just about anything to spend more time with the little boy. Every day he was more and more certain Riley was his child, yet he had to wait until Erin obeyed the court order for the DNA testing. Sure, he could steal a snip of Riley's hair, or at least try to, but that wouldn't hold up in court. Everything had to be done properly. Every *t* crossed and every *i* dotted.

"Oh, no. I couldn't expect you to do that—you have your own work to do. Besides, you don't have any experience with babies, do you?" She must have seen the stricken look that crossed his features because she hastened to add, "I'm sorry, that was careless of me."

"It's okay," he reassured her. "But still, if I'm not busy and you want to get things done around the place while Riley's awake, I don't see why I couldn't mind him here for you."

"Seriously?" Erin gave him a cheeky grin that made his heart do a crazy flip-flop in his chest. "And if he fills his diaper?"

"I'll do my best," Sam said stoically. He'd have to do his best if Riley did turn out to be his. He had every intention of being a major part of his son's life.

"I'll think about it," Erin said with another smile.

"You're beautiful when you smile like that," Sam said, without thinking. "Well, you're beautiful all the time, but especially when you smile."

A flush of pink warmed her cheeks. "Thank you. I don't remember the last time anyone said anything like that."

"Then I'll remember to tell you more often," he said, his voice pitched very low.

He drained the last of his whiskey in one swallow and rose to his feet.

"I should probably be off, see if I can retrieve that file. Thanks for the company, and thanks for the drink."

Erin stood, as well. "You're welcome, anytime. I'd forgotten how civilized it could feel sitting and sharing a drink with someone."

She smiled again and Sam felt the impact of it all the way to his gut. He took a step closer to her, captured one of her hands in his and lifted it to his mouth.

"Being civilized is vastly underrated," he said, lifting his eyes to meet hers as his lips pressed against her skin.

He saw her pupils dilate at his touch, her nostrils flare ever so slightly. He didn't let go of her hand as he lifted his head, instead he pulled her closer, into the circle of his embrace. She didn't protest, not one bit, not even when he lowered his face to hers and caught her lips with his own, relishing the sensation of her body against his.

The round firmness of her breasts pressed against his chest, the soft swell of her belly against the firmer planes of his own, the cradle of her hips against his arousal. Sam groaned. This was crazy. Crazy and completely impossible to resist. Her mouth parted beneath his, her tongue gently flicking against his own. God, he couldn't get enough of the taste of her. He plundered her mouth, angling his head so they all but fused together.

His hands shoved under the edge of her T-shirt, pushing the soft fabric up to expose her skin. Skin that was soft, enticing. Warm, when he'd felt cold to his very soul for so long. He lifted the garment higher, breaking their kiss only long enough to pull it over her head and to let it drop on the floor behind her.

Erin opened her eyes and he was struck by the vulnerability he saw there in their dark brown depths. He said the first thing that came to mind.

"I want you, Erin. Tell me to stop now and I will. Or tell me you want me, too."

He felt the tremors that ran through her body and took a half step back, giving her the space he thought she needed. She could turn him down. He wouldn't hold that against her. Sure, he'd be uncomfortable, physically, but he wasn't the kind of guy who forced himself on a beautiful woman no matter how much his desire for her threatened to consume him.

"I…I want you, too," she said softly.

In fact, she'd spoken so softly he wasn't entirely sure he'd heard what he wanted, or what she'd actually meant.

"Erin—"

"I want you, Sam," she said, more firmly this time. "But I don't know what you want out of this, or from me."

He felt his heart squeeze. He knew exactly what she meant. They were each so raw with emotion in their own ways.

"I don't know either," honesty forced him to admit. "But I do know that I've felt alone and empty for too long. I think you know what I mean, how it feels." He paused and felt his pulse skip a beat when she nodded slowly, her eyes locked with his. "I think we can make that emptiness go away, for a while, together. We deserve that, don't we?"

He watched as she pressed her lips together, as if weighing her options before giving him the answer his body begged for.

"And in the morning?" she asked. "What then?"

"I won't think any less of you, Erin. I can promise you that. I haven't been able to get you out of my mind since we kissed last week. I know you felt something then, just as I did. You even said it was what was right for us at the time. And so is this."

He took one of her hands in his and laid it flat against his chest. Could she feel his heart leaping about in there as he did? Could she feel that she did this to him? Turned him from a man intent on escaping from the world, an analytical software designer and developer, into someone who was now ruled by baser instinctive needs and emotions?

Her fingers curled beneath his, her grip tightening on his shirt. She was shaking in earnest now. Had he pushed her too far? Destroyed the delectable closeness they'd only just begun to explore?

"Kiss me again," she whispered. "Make the emptiness go away."

Eight

Erin felt as if she'd just stepped off a precipice, as if she was falling, falling with no idea of how hard the jolt might be when she reached the bottom. But then Sam's lips closed on hers and she could only hope that with him her landing would be safe, secure. She wrapped her arms about his neck and let her body cleave to the length of his.

Everything about him felt good, right. So right she wanted to drop to the carpet right here, right now, with him in her arms and explore in depth just how good it was. But she didn't want their first time to be so elemental. Not while she still held on to at least one rational thought in her head. Instead, she broke their kiss, closing her eyes momentarily at the tiny sensation of loss that swirled through her at the lack of contact, Then, taking his hand, she led him to her bedroom.

She'd turned the sheets down earlier and had left

only a stained-glass lamp turned on at her bedside. The muted jewel-like colors cast a gentle, enticing glow about the room.

She closed the door behind them, cocooning them in a private space in time. Somewhere they could explore the intensity of the attraction between them—the sheer need that arose every time they'd been together. A need they could plunder and delight in, and which could chase away the shadows that lingered in their hearts.

Erin reached for Sam's shirt, tugging it free of his jeans and forcing her shaking fingers to painstakingly undo each button from top to bottom. Inch by inch she revealed the smooth expanse of his chest, the dark nipples that were as rigid as her own, his taut belly and the fine smattering of hair that arrowed behind the waistband of his jeans. She pushed the shirt off his shoulders, leaving his upper torso bare to her gaze. She looked her fill, tracing the lines of his physique with fingers that became more sure of their touch the lower they traveled.

He gasped as she brushed her hand over the erection trapped behind his zipper. She smiled a little, enjoying the pure feminine knowledge that he was this way for her, that he wanted her as much as she wanted him. The anticipation was both a delight and a torment. They would be wonderful together, she knew that as instinctively as she knew the sun would rise each day. But just how wonderful? Would they blaze like a fiery comet through the night sky, or would they simmer and burn like a slow-growing flame?

Her hands fumbled at his belt, and then at his zipper, carefully releasing the pressure against his arousal and easing his jeans down his long legs. In the soft lighting she caught a glimpse of a long scar running the length of Sam's thigh and she felt a moment's sorrow for the injury that had caused such a permanent reminder. But she didn't linger long over the thought, instead rising once again, skimming her hands up the outside of his legs and then guiding them in toward the straining fabric of his boxer briefs. She grazed her nails over the knitted cotton, relishing the groan he emitted. His hands shot to her arms, stilling her actions.

"Don't let me spoil this by losing control too soon," he growled, dragging her hands to his hips. "Besides, it's my turn now."

He drifted one finger over the swell of her breasts and Erin's skin shimmered in a scatter of goose bumps. Anticipation thrilled through her body, drawing into a tight knot deep in her belly as he traced the outside edge of her bra cup. For a split second she rued the practicality of the garment, but it was only that tiniest fraction of time before he lifted both hands to slide the straps down over her shoulders and peel the cups of her bra away, exposing her to his concentrated gaze.

She had stretch marks, she knew. The silver striations were a badge of honor to her, but would he see them the same way or would he find them repugnant? She didn't have time to think about the question as he flipped her bra hooks undone and cupped the weight of her in both his hands. His thumbs stroked the tight nubs of her nipples over and over.

"May I kiss you there?" he asked, his voice nothing more than a rasp of emotion.

"Yes." She sighed.

It had been so long since she'd felt like this. Like a woman desired, wanted, needed. As his lips pressed against her flesh she moaned in delight, her fingers threaded through the short strands of his hair, holding him to her, loving every second of the texture of his tongue, the reverence of his lips, the sheer joy of his touch. His broad long-fingered hands splayed across her rib cage, making her feel cherished, special. Feelings she hadn't experienced in so long, if ever.

Emotion threatened to overwhelm her and she dragged several rapid breaths into her aching lungs. Nothing would ruin this night. Nothing. This *was* what was right for them. Tonight, and hopefully for a long time to come.

When Sam undid her jeans, she helped him peel them down her legs and kicked them aside. They were on equal terms, each dressed only in their briefs. She wasn't sure, later, who reached for whom first, but the difference was only a matter of seconds and they were both naked. Erin let her gaze drift over his body, over the torso she'd already come to love the feel of, and hoped soon to enjoy the taste of, too, then lower, to the jutting proof of his desire for her. She slid her fingers around his hard length, relishing the hot silken feel of him. Sam caught his lower lip between his teeth, his sharply indrawn breath a hiss of sound in response to her touch.

"Protection," he ground out. "Let me get my jeans."

A small laugh bubbled from Erin's throat. "You came prepared?" She gave him a firm squeeze and was rewarded with a rumble of pleasure.

"Let's just say, after last week's kiss I thought it might pay to be." He let a teasing smile play around his lips. "I was impressed to discover Connell Lodge really does think of everything. Now I want to return the favor."

His reference to their advertising catch phrase and their determination to make sure their guests would have everything they needed during a stay, made her flush with heat. Was he really saying that he was going to make sure he gave her everything she needed? A mix of desire, and something else, flooded her body. It felt good to be wanted on this level. So very good. She flipped the covers wide open on the bed and lay down on the crisp linens, her skin sensitized to the texture of the cotton against her skin. She couldn't remember the last time she'd lain naked upon the sheets like this. It felt wonderful. *He* made her feel wonderful.

Sam had already sheathed himself and lowered himself to the bed beside her. He trailed one hand from her hips up over her belly to the underside of the swell of her breast, and back down again, each time letting his fingers drift closer to the molten core of her. She knew she was wet for him. Wet and wanting. She squirmed against the sheets, willing his hand closer, striving to feel his touch where her body most wanted it.

When his fingers dipped between the soft folds of her flesh she strained against him and was rewarded when a faint smile crossed his so-intent face. He dipped a little deeper, applying a steady circular pressure to the bead of flesh at her center that already throbbed with an urgent beat. He leaned over her, his lips fusing once more to hers. He drew her lower lip into his mouth, suckling on the plump flesh, his tongue imitating the movement of his fingers across that oh-so-sensitive spot.

Then shards of light speared through her, her climax hitting her body, swift and intense. A sharp keening sound escaped her throat as she rode the waves of pleasure—a pleasure so sure, so powerful that all thought abandoned her, leaving only sensation. She was still shaking in the aftermath when she felt Sam gather her to him, anchoring her to his warmth, his strength. The ultimate security of his embrace.

Erin's heartbeat slowly returned to normal and she became aware of the moisture on her cheeks. She'd wept when she'd orgasmed? She'd never had that kind of reaction before. Mind you, she'd never felt quite like... *that* before.

"You okay?" Sam asked, his voice deep and steady.

"You have no idea," she said, shifting so she could smile at him, reassure him that there was no sorrow in the tears she'd unknowingly spent.

Erin cupped his face with her hand and stroked away his concern. In that second, she knew she'd fallen irrevocably in love with Sam Thornton. It wasn't the pleasure he'd brought her, although that was so welcome she wondered if she could ever settle for less. But it was his care, his consideration. Everything about him made her warm inside. A precious sensation, indeed, after months of being in the cold. Of functioning simply because she had to.

In light of her private admission, it was the most natural thing in the world to ease her body over his, to straddle his hips and to begin to lavish upon his body some of the attention he'd delivered to hers. To show him, even though she wasn't yet brave enough to tell him, exactly how he made her feel. And then, as he trembled beneath her touch, to position his swollen flesh at her centre, to lower herself slowly on his length. A deep aftershock of pleasure rippled through her as she took him inside her, welcoming him into her body, into her very soul.

She rocked against him, and felt his answering thrust. Again and again and yet again until she was lost in a blur of stimulation, conscious only of the man beneath her and the rising tide of pleasure that swelled from that point where they joined. And then the ecstasy peaked, for him and for her, sending them both cascading into a rolling eruption of bliss so sweet she thought she might pass out from it.

Erin collapsed on Sam's chest, their bodies now both slick with perspiration, their breathing labored, their hearts beating frantically, yet as one. As she gave herself over to the darkness, one thought filtered through her shattered mind. The emptiness that Sam had talked about earlier, and that had resonated so strongly with her, was gone.

She must have slept for half an hour or so. When she awoke her body still hummed with the residue of satisfaction. She stirred, realizing that at some stage during her slumber Sam had carefully moved her from on top of him to his side. He must have left the bed, too, however briefly, to dispense with the condom. Now, as she shifted slightly, he adjusted the strong curve of one arm around her to pull her more tightly to him.

This close, she was aware of every aspect of him. Of the shadow of his unshaven cheeks, of the way that the serious lines that usually bracketed his mouth and furrowed his brow during the day—lines that spoke of pain and unhappiness—had now relaxed into smoothness. Even of the scent of him, a mixture of warm skin and spice and essential male, sent her senses into a spiral of heightened consciousness, as if she was attuned to him and him alone.

She wanted to know him better, deeper, more. She already had a handle on what foods and drinks he enjoyed, and over the past week he'd talked a bit about growing up in New Zealand and his move to San Francisco, but to her, all that was peripheral. Suddenly, it was vital to know what made him laugh, what drove him each day—what made him happiest. What made him sad. She already knew losing his wife had plunged him into a dark place. Her hand drifted along his thigh, feeling again the ridge of tissue that still looked newly healed.

And it wasn't his only scar, she noticed in the faded light cast by the bedside lamp. There were others. A neat line, still bearing traces of stitch marks, crossed his abdomen. Smaller, faint silver strikes that she hadn't noticed before marked his forehead, and another one on his jaw—but it was more noticeable for the fact that no stubble grew there.

"Do I pass muster?" Sam asked, his voice a deep rumble by her ear.

"You're beautiful." She said it simply but she meant it with every beat of her heart.

She felt him shake his head. "Not beautiful, Erin. Never that."

"I beg to differ," she said, propping herself up on one elbow. She coasted her hand over the scars on his abdomen and his leg. "These are just marks that show the path of your journey so far."

"They're reminders of the selfish and arrogant man I used to be. That's all."

"I didn't know that man. But I'm getting to know the one you are now, and I like him. A whole lot."

Sam lifted a hand and cupped her face. "That's good, because I like you, too. A whole lot."

She smiled at him, feeling her heart swell in her chest at his words. "Tell me about your injuries, Sam. Tell me about this one." She bent her head to tenderly press a kiss against the scar below his rib cage.

"Lacerated spleen. It won't be a problem if I'm ever in another wreck," he said drily, although Erin sensed the underlying anger at himself in his words. "I don't have it anymore."

"And this?" She repeated the kiss with the scar on his jaw.

"My cellphone, oddly enough. Funny thing when your car is forced to stop rapidly. You and everything else in it don't." He shifted his hand to rest on his thigh. "And this was a compound fracture of my femur. A bone infection, post surgery, ensured my stay in hospital was longer than either I or the medical staff were happy with."

"Not a good patient?"

"Not patient, period," he said bluntly. "Too much time to think about what choices I should have made that day, rather than the ones I did. I learned a lot about myself while I was in hospital, and I didn't like most of it. Eventually I decided, if I had to survive, I had to change. I will never again put my work or myself before my family."

There was a steely undertone to his voice now that resonated with Erin. She knew exactly how he felt. Nothing and no one would get between her and her son. Ever.

"I'm sorry you had to go through all that," she whispered, stroking her hand across his belly with feather-light movements.

His recovery must have been tough. The fact that he hadn't given up on it was a strong measure of the man, and how far he'd come since that awful day. Dare she begin to hope that the rest of his journey might be with her?

Sam lay there, his thoughts churning. Making love with Erin tonight had been a temptation he simply couldn't resist. He wasn't ready for this, for the feelings that being with her aroused in him, for wanting her the way he had—the way he still did. His feelings for her went beyond the physical attraction they so clearly shared. It was something he hadn't anticipated and he had no preselected mechanism to cope with this resurgence of emotions.

He'd thought he'd learned to shut himself down. To be the quintessential iceman as far as his feelings were concerned. He knew what it was like to go through the wringer. Sentiment wasn't something he welcomed into his life anymore. And yet, with Erin, and with Riley, he'd found an awakening of hope. A small kernel of a dream he'd once had. A dream he'd expected to share with Laura but to which, in light of his role in her death, he'd decided he was no longer entitled.

He still didn't believe he deserved to find happiness, but fate had thrown him a second chance with the possibility that Riley might be his son. Was it possible that, together with Erin and Riley, he could have that chance of a family that he'd thought he'd lost forever? Could he reach for the happiness he so wanted, yet deep down didn't believe he deserved?

Maybe he could.

He reached down to his jeans on the floor next to the bed, sliding the other condom he'd put in there—just in case—into his hand. Whatever happiness there was to be taken, it began now—here, with Erin. The ice in his veins had begun to thaw, leaving in its wake a hot drumming need to bury himself in Erin's softness, her welcoming warmth.

He rolled over her, loving the sizzle of sensitivity that sparked between them, skin to skin. She was so responsive, so giving.

This time as they made love, he took his time. Bringing to her the crest of a peak, then letting her slowly dip before he allowed her to launch again. His need was strung so tight, by the time he ripped open the foil packet he'd shoved under the pillow he almost messed up putting the condom on. But then finally he was there, his erection arrowed straight toward her body.

Their joining was slow as he fought to prolong every second, his hands holding her hips when she would have pushed against him, enveloping him in her heat. The pleasure-pain of holding back, of teasing her as he withdrew only to enter her again, slowly, oh, so slowly, took every ounce of concentration he had. Concentration that went flying to the four corners of the room the minute he allowed his body to penetrate her fully. She closed around him, holding him to her, tight. Her arms snaked around his body, pulling him down against her, length for length. And as he began to rock gently within her he knew they had no beginning, they had no end. They just had each other in this perfect moment in time.

Nine

Sam wiped away the remnants of shaving foam from his jaw and looked at himself in the bathroom mirror. He could barely keep a smile off his face these days. Over the past two weeks, since the first night he and Erin had made love, their days and nights had slid into an easy rhythm. One punctuated only by the day she and Riley had gone to her lawyer's office for the supervised sample taking. Knowing where they were going, and why, had driven him crazy for the couple of hours they were gone. But now things were really in motion, his kind of motion.

He hated waiting, but he knew that each day would just bring him closer to the result he hoped would be music to his ears. And, in the meantime, he'd begun to allow himself to feel happy, to feel a measure of hope for the future.

Every day was brighter, better—something he would

never have believed possible—and he could feel the bond between himself and Riley growing stronger. He genuinely loved the little boy. He'd tried to hold back, in case everything just blew right up in his face again, but every day he saw in Riley something of himself, or his family, that underscored his paternity. Now all he needed was the clinical confirmation and he could set new plans in motion. Plans that included Erin and Riley in his future. A future he never dreamed he'd want again, or stood a good chance to have.

He turned away from the mirror just as he heard his cellphone begin to ring from where he'd tossed it onto the bed in his room. A bed he hadn't slept in for a while. And there it was again, the smile.

Tightening the towel he'd wrapped around his waist after his shower, he limped across to the bed and cast a glance at the caller ID. A rush of adrenaline flooded his entire body with an icy chill. David Fox, his lawyer. He accepted the call and barked a greeting.

"And a good morning to you, too," David said smoothly.

Sam could hear the smile in the other man's voice. "Get to the point, Dave."

"Break out the cigars. It's a positive match."

Sam couldn't speak. There was a lump in his throat the size of Mount Rushmore. He slowly sank to the edge of the bed.

"Sam? You okay, bud?"

He swallowed then coughed a little. "There's no doubt?" His voice came out a little rough.

"No doubt whatsoever. He's your son."

Sam could barely begin to assimilate the news. From the moment he'd been notified about the potential error at the fertility clinic he'd been hoping against hope that

Riley Connell was his little boy. Now he had incontro-
vertible proof. He was a father. Riley was his son.

"What happens next?" Sam asked, still a little shaky.

"We approach his mother with the findings and suggest that a joint custody arrangement be reached. If she's
reluctant to cooperate we can launch action to ensure
that your rights as the child's father are met."

"Wait on that for a while, okay? I...I just need a couple of days first."

How would she take the news, he wondered. If he
was the one to tell her—and along with that to share
with her his feelings for both her and Riley—would
that make a difference?

"Sure, if you're certain that's what you want."

"It is," Sam said, his voice firm now. He didn't bother
to give any further explanation.

Dave had no idea of what he was up to, or that he'd
hired a private investigator to find Erin Connell in the
first place. He doubted the man would have approved.
Whatever, it didn't matter one bit. He'd wanted to see
the child, had wanted to meet the child's mother. He'd
done that—and more. What happened next would need
to be very carefully orchestrated.

"Okay then. I'll wait for your instructions."

Sam disconnected the call and got to his feet. A part
of him wanted to race downstairs—well, as much as
he could race with his blasted leg—and give Erin the
news. To reveal who he was and what that meant to
them as a family. A family. The moniker reverberated
through his mind.

His family.

Erin was humming in the kitchen as she packed the
picnic basket she was about to take out to the boat.

Today she planned a very special outing. Before she sent the boat away to the storage facility she'd decided to take Sam out on the lake for a day. Just the two of them. Sasha had happily agreed to babysit Riley here at the house and Erin had made a sumptuous lunch. She'd also made sure the small stateroom on board held every possible accoutrement they might need during their day. All going well, she didn't plan on them being back until shortly before dark.

Her whole body buzzed with anticipation as she mentally ticked off the list she had in the back of her mind, and a tiny thrill of excitement purred through her as she thought about the delights she had planned. After taking Sam on a scenic tour of the lake, and maybe some fishing with the day license she'd secured, she planned to bring him back into the cove, anchoring just the other side of the outcrop that would give them privacy from both the lake and the house.

There, she planned to show him, in word and deed, exactly how much she loved him. Yes, today she would declare her feelings. It was time and it felt right, so right the joy teemed through her.

"You sound happy."

Sam's voice came from behind her, making her jump. How he still managed to do that astounded her. His arms locked around her waist from behind and he kissed the nape of her neck, sending a shiver of delight through her body. She turned in the circle of his arms with a smile on her face and brushed a kiss against his lips.

"Good morning. And if I sound happy, it's because I am."

She gave him a good look. She felt that over the past few weeks she'd begun to get to know him pretty well, but there was something different about him today. It was as if he pulsed with a new energy. Something that shone from his eyes and lightened his features.

"I hope you weren't planning on working today," she continued, "because I have plans to kidnap you and take you away for the day."

"Sounds intriguing." He smiled back. "I'm open to persuasion. Riley will enjoy a day out, too, I'm sure."

"I've made other arrangements for him today. Sasha will be looking after him here at the lodge." She leaned closer and punctuated each of her next few words with a kiss. "I. Want. You. All. To. Myself."

She was tingling all over when she pulled away to finish checking the contents of the basket. She hefted it up off the table.

"Let me help you with that," Sam said, stepping forward to take the basket from her.

"No, it's okay. I'm just going to take this out to the boat and then I'll be back."

"You know it's okay to accept help from other people from time to time." He said it softly but some of the light and energy that had surrounded him seemed to fade a little.

Erin wondered if she'd hurt his feelings by not accepting his help. Sure, he'd been injured, but he wasn't incapacitated by any means. But that wasn't it. Not for her, anyway. She was used to looking out for herself. Even with her marriage she'd maintained a measure of distance, of independence that she hadn't been prepared to relinquish. Probably a hangover from the days when she'd been reliant on others for everything, and nothing had been forthcoming. She gave her head a small shake. She didn't want to go there, not today.

She smiled up at him. "I know, but I want everything about this to be a surprise treat for you. How can I be sure you won't peek and spoil the surprise if I let you take this out to the boat for me?"

His features softened and he gave her a crooked smile. "Nice cover," he said. "I'm inclined to argue but let's leave it at that for now."

"Look, if you want to help, can you keep an eye on Riley for me? He's on his play mat in my sitting room."

With her free hand, she unclipped the baby monitor from her hip and put it on the kitchen table then shifted the weight of the basket on her arm.

"Sure, no problem."

"Great, thanks. I'll be back in a minute. Sash should be here soon and then we can head out."

Sam didn't wait for her to leave the house. He went straight through to the sitting room to where Riley was having fun with the play gym set up over his mat. His heart gave that now-familiar squeeze when he saw the little boy. Little boy? Hell—his *son*.

"Hello, little man," he said, lowering himself to the floor beside the baby.

Riley squirmed on the mat, pumping his arms and legs in excitement.

Sam laughed, he couldn't help it. Looking at Riley, *knowing* he was his son, filled a missing piece inside of him that had threatened to overwhelm him without him even realizing it. He reached for the little boy, scooting him out from under the play gym and scooping him up to sit on his stomach. Riley clutched at the hair on his forearms and gave him a gummy grin, then gabbled a run of baby-speak.

Sam couldn't take his eyes off Riley. Now almost five months old, Sam had missed a whole lot of his early development, but as he lay there he promised himself he wouldn't miss a minute more than absolutely necessary. He'd wanted to argue with Erin back there in the kitchen, to insist that whatever they did today include Riley as well, but he couldn't tip his hand too early. He would reveal who he was in relation to Riley in good time. She probably wouldn't take the news well, especially when she found out that he'd had her tracked down to jump ahead of the slow-turning wheels of the legal system.

But it was worth it. Every second had been worth it. And he and Erin were on the precipice of something special, he knew it. They'd make a great family, raising Riley together. She was falling in love with him, he felt it with every glance, every special thing she did for him. It wasn't arrogance that made him feel the strength of her emotions toward him. It was an intense and deep-seated awareness. An awareness that he, too, was developing the same level of feelings toward her.

Acknowledging that had been more than half the battle for Sam. After Laura, he hadn't expected or wanted to love again, and his life had become bitter and empty for that lack within it. Now, he could feel a wholly different love. One no less special than what he'd shared with Laura, but one that was enriched by what both he and Erin had been through, what they'd endured to get where they were today.

Beneath his hands, Sam relished the feel of Riley's sturdy little body, of the miracle of the cells that had developed and grown and made the whole child. Of the gift that this tiny person was here, in part, because of him. It was an overwhelming responsibility, one Sam looked forward to bearing upon his shoulders for the rest of his life.

He tickled Riley's tummy and was rewarded with a belly laugh that made him laugh in return.

"You are the most amazing little boy," he said out loud, picking the baby up and dangling him over him.

Riley laughed again, reaching for Sam's face, his plump little fingers patting his cheeks as if in agreement with what he'd just said.

Erin came in through the doorway. "Well, you two look like quite the mutual admiration society."

Sam smiled back, "And the problem is?"

"No problem," she replied, lowering herself to the floor beside them. "You look good together."

Which was only right and natural, Sam thought, but she didn't know that. Not yet, anyway.

Outside they heard the sound of Sasha's car pulling up and then the back door opening as she let herself in.

"We're through here," Erin called.

"Hi, I'm sorry I was running a little late," Sasha said breathlessly as she came through the door. "One of the girls was a bit under the weather this morning. Tony's staying home with her. Oh, hello." She cut off abruptly when she realized Erin wasn't alone.

"Hi," he said briefly. "I hope your daughter will be okay."

"You should have called. I could've changed our plans," Erin protested.

"No, I wouldn't hear of it. Seriously, she'll be fine," Sasha assured them. "There's a nasty cold going around at the moment. Rest and fluids and her dad's devoted attention and she'll be as good as new in no time. Besides, it'll be good for her dad to play nursemaid for a change."

Erin laughed. "He's a great father. You're very lucky."

"No, it's not lucky. Parenting is a two-person job

most of the time and it's all about sharing the load in our house."

"I agree," Sam said, straightening up from the floor, now holding Riley against his chest with one arm. "That's the way it should be."

He looked forward to when he could openly claim his place as Riley's father. He planned to be fully hands-on with his care and decisions about his future.

"You two had better get going," Sasha suggested, "and let me do what I came here to do." She put her hands out to Riley who happily went into her arms.

"Thanks for coming, Sash," Erin said. "I do appreciate it."

"Hey, you know I love it. One kid at a time is such a luxury. Now, get going before the day disappears on you."

"Come on then." Erin turned to Sam and gave him a gentle nudge toward the door. "You heard the woman. We'll see you later, Sasha. Bye, Riley-bear."

Erin gave Riley a kiss on his cheek then frowned.

"Does he feel a bit warm to you?" she asked her friend.

Sasha felt his forehead and shook her head. "He's fine. Don't worry about us. Go and enjoy yourselves."

"You have my cell number, right? Call me if there are any problems, okay?"

Sam felt a surge of frustration that he didn't have the right to be consulted as to Riley's well-being. The emotion was tempered with the knowledge that Erin wouldn't willingly leave her son if she genuinely thought something was amiss. Even so, it wasn't easy to just walk away when all he wanted to do was cherish every minute with their boy. Anticipation for whatever surprise Erin had prepared for him was the only thing that propelled him out of the room.

As they reached the kitchen Sam asked, "Is there anything I need to bring?"

"Maybe a light jacket. It can get quite cold out on the water, even on a lovely clear day like this."

"Okay, I'll meet you at the end of the pier in a couple of minutes."

"Good. I'll go get the motor started up."

Sam went upstairs as quickly as he could manage and grabbed a windbreaker from his wardrobe. On his way back out, he couldn't quite rid himself of the urge to see his son one more time before they left. He popped his head into the sitting room where Sasha was seated in one of the deep armchairs, reading to Riley.

"You're off now then?" Sasha asked, looking up from the book.

"Yeah, you two have a good day and don't hesitate to call if there are any problems with Riley."

"I promise," Sasha said, giving him a strange look.

Maybe he'd overplayed it, he thought as he let himself out the back door and headed toward the pier. But when it came to his child, he'd do whatever it took to keep him safe, no matter what anyone thought.

Ten

Motoring back toward Connell Bay, Erin took a moment to enjoy her surroundings. It had been idyllic on the lake, although the breeze across the water had been chilly. For now, Sam was at the helm and Erin took a moment to relish the sight of him. So tall, so strong, so entirely masculine. He looked happier than he had when he'd arrived at Connell Lodge, and the outing today had thrown extra color into his cheeks. God, how would she cope when he had to return to San Francisco?

Her heart was utterly and irrevocably wrapped up in this man. Being alone with him today had only underscored her growing feelings for him. There'd been a sense of togetherness, of unity, that she'd never experienced with anyone else before. Today had been a gift of time.

"Where do you want to anchor?" Sam asked as he dropped the engine speed back to a slow cruise.

"Just a little farther." She stood close behind him, one hand on his shoulder, the other pointing to the spot she had in mind for their picnic. "There's a natural shelf just there. It's the best place to drop anchor."

He deftly maneuvered the vessel to where she'd indicated and activated the winch to release the anchor to settle onto the lake floor below them. Once he was satisfied they were secured, he shut the motor off.

"That was great. I'd forgotten how much I enjoyed boating."

"You did really well. You had a boat back home in New Zealand?"

"Oh, yeah. Similar to this beauty. I miss it, actually. I might look into getting a berth and something like this when I'm back in San Francisco."

She felt the words as if they were barbed arrows fired straight at her chest. She forced a bright smile to her face, determined not to think about that time when he might be leaving and to make the most of their time today.

"Hungry?" she asked, heading into the cabin where she'd stowed the picnic basket.

"Definitely. Do you need a hand?"

"Sure. I put a bottle of wine in the refrigerator. Can you grab it and the glasses from the rack above? I'll set the food out."

Erin brushed against him as they moved about in the compact galley, her senses swinging into high alert as they did so. She wanted nothing more than to wrestle him down onto one of the banquettes and have her wicked way with him right now, but she'd planned everything about this day so carefully, she wasn't about to give in to rash impulses now. A tiny smile played around her lips as she thought about what she had in mind.

"Care to share the joke?" Sam asked, bringing the wine and glasses to the table she'd set up on the back deck of the launch.

"Soon," she promised.

"Soon, huh? I am intrigued. Are you going to give me a hint?"

She shook her head. "Nothing you won't enjoy, later."

He laughed and reached out to cup her face with one large warm hand. She turned her face in toward him, kissing his palm.

"There, that'll have to suffice for now."

"I can't wait," he said with one brow raised.

Heat suffused her cheeks. She could barely wait either, but anticipation was half of the fun today. They had time to really enjoy one another, and they would. She quickly laid out the food she'd packed and put together the fixings she'd brought for a smoked chicken and papaya salad, her much-loved buttermilk dressing, crusty French bread and a selection of sliced fruit to enjoy after lunch. Sam poured them each a small glass of the perfectly chilled sauvignon blanc and lifted his in a toast.

"To the perfect hostess," he said, clinking his glass with hers.

"To the perfect guest," she answered, lifting her glass and taking a sip of the crisp wine.

He didn't take his eyes off her as she drank and she felt the hum that had been simmering through her body since early this morning step up a gear. He didn't say a word, but she knew exactly what he was thinking as his eyes dropped to her lips. She licked them, savoring the taste of the wine, but savoring the expression on his face even more. His pupils dilated, his cheeks flushed with a heat that had nothing to do with the breeze or the sun they'd enjoyed so far today.

A tingle ran up her spine and she averted her gaze, concentrating instead on picking up her fork and sampling the salad. Sam eventually did the same.

The afternoon light was stunning, and the situation glorious. The soothing lap of the water against the hull of the boat was sinfully relaxing and they were the only boat in the bay. One of the advantages of the narrow entry into Connell Cove was that many boaters missed it completely while out on the lake. They ate for a while in companionable silence. Erin refused Sam's offer to top up her wine. She really wanted her wits about her for what she had planned for the balance of their day together.

Sam shifted in his seat and she couldn't miss the swiftly masked expression of pain that crossed his features.

"How's your leg holding out on the boat?"

"Okay," he said, but she could see he was hurting.

"Does massage help?"

"Sometimes," he admitted.

"How about I give you a massage? Have you had enough to eat?"

She raised her eyes to his again, and saw an answering flare in his. There was no question he was hungry, but that hunger had nothing to do with food.

"Here," she said, holding out her hand. "Come into the cabin and I'll see what I can do to make you more comfortable."

She led him down the four steps into the boat's interior and toward the large V-shaped berth in the forward section.

"Now, let's get you more comfortable," she said with a suggestive smile.

"Whatever the lady wants," Sam replied in kind and shucked off his sweater over his head then kicked off his shoes before dropping his jeans to the floor. "Will this do?"

Erin ran a hand down his chest, across his abdomen and lower, skimming the growing hardness in his boxer briefs. "For now," she said.

She raised her hand to his chest and gave him a playful shove toward the berth, its wide expanse not unlike the California king-size beds she had in the guest rooms at the lodge. Once he was lying down, she stripped down to her underwear, thankful that she still had a matching set that was both sexy and managed to fit her. She climbed onto the bed next to him.

"Very nice," Sam commented as she rose to her knees on the bed and took the massage oil from the built-in shelving where she'd stowed it earlier.

He reached for her, his hands skimming her waist and up her rib cage, sending tiny shimmers of electricity across her skin. She grabbed his hands and drew them away from her body. She wanted today to be all about him and how she felt about him.

"Just relax," she whispered as she placed his hands on either side of his body. "Let me do all the work this time."

He lowered his eyelids, gazing at her with a deep and dark sensual look that sent a thrill of excitement through her. One thing she'd noted about his lovemaking in the past week was that he was a giver, not a taker. He liked to be in control, to pace their activity, to ensure that she was left fully satisfied in every way. It had been incredible. She'd never known anything, or anyone, like that before. Someone so generous and unselfish. He more than deserved the same in kind.

Erin twisted the cap off the bottle of massage oil, and poured a little into her hand before tucking the bottle safely back into the shelving unit. The essential-oil-infused liquid warmed quickly in her hands and she smoothed it over Sam's injured leg in long, smooth strokes.

"Tell me if that pressure is too much."

He merely grunted as she deepened the pressure, using all the skills she'd read about while preparing for today. Mindful not to do more harm than good, she poured a little more oil in her hands and worked on his other leg as well, before moving higher on his torso.

Her hands were tingling with the sensation of the smooth oil coasting over his warm skin and she was aware of his growing arousal as she hovered over his body. His growing arousal *and* her own. She stroked her hands over his shoulders, relishing the strength beneath her touch, before massaging down each of his arms and finishing with his hands.

"All good?" she asked, trying for a sexy drawl.

"Mmm-hmm," he murmured, still watching her from beneath those half-lidded eyes.

"It's about to get better," she promised, skimming her hands back down over his body and to the waistband of his briefs. "Lift your hips a little," she commanded.

As he did she eased his briefs over his hips, and down his long legs. She tossed them to the floor and ran her fingers up the insides of his legs.

"Now for the fun part," she whispered, and bent down to blow warm air over his straining flesh.

She caught his erection in one hand, loving the silk-on-steel feel of his skin. Her hands were still slick from the massage oil and she slid them from base to tip and down again, squeezing gently as she did so. He groaned beneath her touch, a flush of heat suffusing his chest and throat.

"You like that?" she teased.

"You know I do, wretched woman," he ground out in response.

"How about this?"

She bent lower, and used the tip of her tongue to trace the rim of the swollen head of his penis. He jerked at her touch, his hips and thighs tense.

"Yes, that, too," he growled.

"Good. Then you'll like this, too, I hope."

She closed her lips around him, swirling her tongue around and around and sucking at his engorged flesh as if he were a feast laid out before a starving person. With one hand she cupped his sac, gently massaging him, while with the other she stroked him in rhythm with the actions of her mouth, her tongue, her lips. She felt him begin to tremble beneath her, felt his fingers catch in her hair. And then she felt him break, tasted the rush of his climax, heard the guttural cry wrenched from deep inside him. His body spasmed beneath her, his hips bowing upward as the waves of pleasure shook him until he was spent.

She slowed her motions, eventually releasing his softening length to fall against his belly. She stretched out alongside him, one arm tracing the outline of his ribs as his breathing, at first ragged, eventually calmed to a normal rhythm. Sam rolled onto his side to face her and reached to pull her hard against his body before capturing her lips in a kiss that was hard and deep and wet. Every nerve in her body responded and she felt herself grow damp between her legs even as tension coiled tight in the hidden recesses of her body.

"Your turn, I believe," he rasped against her lips, rolling over her body before propping himself up on knees that straddled her hips.

"No, Sam, you don't have to. I wanted to give you that, to show you—"

Her voice broke off. Now the moment was here, the words she had wanted so much to share with him still lingered on her tongue, afraid to make it out into the wide world where they could be used against her. Could even hurt her.

"I wanted to show you how much you mean to me," she finished, reaching up to cup his face between her hands, hoping that her eyes showed him the words she was suddenly too frightened to say.

"Erin, don't you understand? The feeling is entirely mutual." Sam sighed and lowered himself so that their faces were only inches apart, his gray eyes holding her with a gaze so intense she was afraid to look away. "I never expected to feel like this again, with anyone. This is a gift that we share."

He kissed her again, this time so tenderly she felt the burn of tears at the back of her eyes. She fought them back. She would not cry. This was a gift, just as he said, and she wasn't prepared to waste it.

This time, when Sam pulled back, she remained silent, emitting sound only when she was helpless to hold it back as he traced the shape of her body with his lips and his tongue. When he undid the clasp of her bra, she felt her breasts spill out into his eager hands, sensed the heat of his mouth before she felt it on the tender, sensitive buds of her nipples. First one, then the other, each laved with enough attention that she was squirming against him, lifting her hips to his in silent entreaty.

His shaft was a rigid spear against her body and she tried to reach for him, to stroke him, but he grasped her wrists and pulled her hands high over her head, leaving her prone to his gaze and his touch. She opened her eyes and saw in his a new reverence as he looked his fill of her before continuing his tortuous path, kissing and tasting her torso, lower and lower until she felt the warmth of his breath through the scrap of lace at her hips.

When he lowered his mouth to her, tasting her through her panties, she nearly screamed. Every nerve in her body tightened to an almost unbearable tension. He released her hands so he could tug at the tiny garment, sliding it down her legs and off her before she realized what he was doing, and then his mouth was there again, his tongue circling her clit in exquisite torment before he sealed his lips around her and suckled. The orgasm that broke through her body was a tidal wave of sensation that sent burst after burst of pleasure pulsing through her.

By the time she gathered her scattered senses Sam was lying beside her again, a half smile on his face.

"You like that?" he teased, using her earlier words right back at her.

She laughed, the sound filling her and expanding out into the cabin around them. God, he made her so incredibly, deeply happy.

"Yeah, I did," she answered, grinning widely. "And, feel free to let it go completely to your head, you have every right to look so darn smug."

They lay together in the filtered golden light that beamed softly through the opaque skylight above them and Erin knew she'd never felt so happy. Never believed she deserved to feel this good. When Sam leaned over and kissed her again, her body quickened almost immediately, hungry for more of what he had to offer. It seemed the more satisfaction she received, the more she craved and the more she wanted to give in return.

"Condom?" Sam asked, pulling away from her just a fraction.

"Right-hand cupboard, there," she pointed.

He reached up and grabbed a foil packet, ripping it open and deftly rolling the protection over his rigid shaft. Positioning himself between her thighs he slowly eased within her, burying himself to the hilt.

"You feel so damn good," he rumbled, his mouth at her throat, his teeth grazing the soft curve where her neck met her shoulder.

Erin grasped him tight with her inner muscles, pulling him as deep within her as she could bear before releasing him again. She was beyond words as he withdrew before sliding home again and again in that most ancient dance of perfection. This time when she climaxed, she felt him tumble with her as, with her hips meeting his every thrust and her inner muscles clamping tight, she wrung both his satisfaction and hers from their bodies.

Sam collapsed on top of her and she wrapped her arms around him, relishing the heavy, sweaty weight of him, sensing the exact moment he slipped from conscious awareness into the oblivion of exhausted slumber. She hooked her legs around his and hugged him with her entire body.

"I love you."

She whispered it ever so faintly she wondered if she'd even said it aloud at all, then closed her eyes and let sleep take her.

Eleven

The persistent chime of her cellphone dragged Erin from her slumber. It stopped briefly, before starting again. Sam shifted his weight so she could get clear of the bed. Naked, she slid the phone from her bag and felt her stomach drop when she saw Sasha's number on the caller display.

"Sasha? I'm sorry I didn't get to the phone earlier, is everything okay?"

In the background she could hear the strident wails of her little boy.

"I'm sorry, Erin. He woke from his afternoon sleep with a slight fever and he's been unhappy ever since. I think it's getting worse, and he keeps tugging at his ear, too. Can you get back soon? I really think he needs to see a doctor."

"Of course. We'll be there in about ten minutes or so, we're not far away."

"Good, do you want me to give him a dose of liquid painkiller? It might help with the fever."

Erin was normally not an advocate of using painkillers with small children, especially not her own small child, but his crying was so piteous she knew they had to offer him some relief.

"Sure, there's a bottle, for emergencies, in the cupboard above the refrigerator. A sterile dropper is in the box with it."

Sasha ended the call to go in search of the medication, leaving Erin standing holding her phone and feeling distraught. Her baby needed her and she'd been out here on the lake taking her pleasure with a man she'd only recently met. Guilt threatened to overwhelm her.

"Erin? Is Riley okay?" Sam was already sliding off the bed and reaching for his clothing.

"No, he's not. Sasha said he woke with a fever and—" she felt her throat close up with anxiety "—he's screaming his head off. He's never like that. Never."

"Here, let me help you with your things. Don't worry, we'll be there soon and we can get him to the doctor. He's in good hands for now."

Guilt sat on her chest like a lead weight. What was it she'd been thinking earlier, about how happy she was? She'd been a fool to embrace it, a fool to think she deserved it. There was always a price to pay. It had been no different when she was younger, it certainly was no different now.

She accepted her underwear from Sam and hastily pulled it on, her hands fumbling at the clasp of her bra. Sam brushed her hands away and capably snapped the front clasp closed and silently handed her T-shirt and jeans to her. She shoved her feet into her shoes, not bothering with her socks as Sam dressed rapidly beside her.

"Don't worry about anything else. We can attend to it later," he said, climbing up the steps that led to the wheel.

Erin stood next to him, frozen with worry, as he capably started the motor, lifted the anchor and carefully pulled away from the spot that had seemed so perfect only a short while ago. Now it was the furthest distance imaginable from her sick baby. They rounded the point and the pier came into view, her home and Riley behind it. As they drew next to the pier she leaped from the boat and hesitated only long enough to tie it off before sprinting for the house.

She burst in through the back door, Riley's cries sharp in the air.

"Oh, thank goodness you're back," Sasha said, her voice quavering. "I know I've had three of my own and all that but there are times when only a baby's mother will do."

"It's okay, Sasha. It's nothing you did."

She reached out her arms to Riley and scooped him close to her. His screams quieted down to sobs, but his crying didn't stop. "Shh, Riley-bear, we'll get you to the doctor, don't worry. They'll make you all better again."

Erin dropped down into a chair, lifted her T-shirt and unsnapped her bra in an attempt to soothe Riley by nursing him, but he wouldn't have any of it. He simply turned his face away and kept on crying.

"What can I do to help?"

Erin turned to the sound of Sam's deep voice beside her.

"Can you get his car seat from the nursery and bring it through?"

"Good idea," Sasha interjected. "And I'll get his diaper bag ready for you, just in case you have to wait at the emergency room. Although with how upset he is, I think they'll hurry you through."

Between the two of them, they gathered everything Erin needed to get Riley to the doctor. Sasha left as Erin was buckling Riley into the baby carrier before carrying him out to the car.

"Have you got everything you need?" Sam asked, coming back inside after putting the diaper bag and Erin's handbag in the car for her.

"I think so." She thought for a minute, next to impossible to do with Riley's distress filling the air. "Car keys! I think I left them in my office. They'll be under some papers I think, on the desk. Can you grab them for me while I secure the car seat?"

"Sure."

Sam had never seen the baby so distressed. It cut him to his core knowing there was little he could do to help. He made his way as quickly as he could to Erin's office and looked around. No obvious sign of the keys, he noted, and reached to pat the papers on her desk. He gave a grim smile. The woman might be almost fanatical about keeping the lodge spick-and-span but she left a lot to be desired when it came to paperwork. It was endearing and reassuring at the same time that she was vulnerable in at least one area of her life. She seemed to handle everything else so capably.

He shifted some papers to one side, sending an envelope falling to the carpet. As he picked it up, he noticed the keys tucked behind another pile of papers at the corner of the desk. He grabbed them and was about to put the envelope back on the desk when he noticed the return address on the back.

It was the facility David had used for the DNA testing they'd recently done on Riley. Why would Erin have had correspondence from them, he wondered. He slid the papers out of the envelope and noted it was dated two weeks ago. His eyes skimmed the details quickly, then again more slowly as he tried to assimilate the words on the page with the confusion in his mind.

She already knew James Connell wasn't Riley's biological father? But why wouldn't she have said anything? Why make *him* wait and go through all that rigmarole of asking further questions and only responding to the requests for testing once the court order came through? A flash of red clouded his vision as a fast-burning anger swelled through him. How dare she have withheld this truth?

What kind of woman did that? He shoved the letter back into the envelope and dropped it back onto the desk. Whatever her reasons, and he had to give her the benefit of the doubt, he wouldn't be able to press her for them now. Right now their most urgent priority was to get Riley to the doctor and find out what, exactly, was wrong.

Erin had Riley secured in his car seat and she rushed to Sam as he exited the back door, pulling it closed behind him and testing to ensure it was locked.

"Here," he said. "The keys."

Erin all but snatched them. She slid into the driver's seat of the car and tried to put the keys in the ignition. Now that his mother wasn't near him, Riley started to scream again, the sound so wretched and heartbreaking that even Sam began to feel close to tears.

To his surprise, Erin slammed a fist on the steering wheel.

"I can't do it," she sobbed, tears now streaming down her face. "I can't drive with him so upset. I need to be back there with him. You'll have to drive us."

Before he could protest, she was out of the seat and tucking herself into the back with Riley.

"Sam! Please, you have to drive us," she implored when he didn't move.

"Erin, you don't understand. I haven't driven since—"

"Sam, we need you. Please." She was sobbing in earnest now.

He gritted his teeth and tried to still the anxiety that now tied his stomach in knots of sheer terror. A cold bead of sweat ran down his spine as he walked around the car and lowered himself into the driver's seat. It hurt to breathe and his muscles felt as if they were locked solid, refusing to obey his mental commands to reach for the key in the ignition and start the car.

He hadn't had a moment's hesitation while out on the boat, yet right now he could barely hold back the bile that rose in his throat, let alone drive this heap of metal and motor—this potential death trap.

"Sam?"

"All right!" he snapped back then instantly wished his words back. "I'm sorry, I'll do it. Just give me a moment."

The fear in Erin's voice tripped a trigger in his brain and with a shaking hand he reached to turn the key. The engine roared to life, making him realize that he had automatically pumped the gas. He snapped his seat belt tight and reached to put the car in gear before letting the emergency brake go. One step at a time, he mentally ticked the boxes.

The car inched slowly forward and Sam found himself fighting back the urge to throw up. In the back of the car Riley's screams had stopped again, and even his crying had subsided a little. In the rearview mirror he noticed Erin was bent over his car seat. She looked up into the mirror, meeting Sam's eyes.

"You can do this, Sam. But you're going to have to go a little faster," she said with a watery smile.

He looked down at the speedometer. Ten miles an hour. He'd have laughed if the situation hadn't been so ridiculously nerve-racking. If the lives of his son and his son's mother didn't depend on how he managed to drive the car.

His fingers curled even tighter on the steering wheel as he applied more pressure to the accelerator. The car jerked forward then slowed as he dragged his foot back again. God, he was a mess. What if he did that up on the road? That awful winding road that led to the nearest town. What if he did something stupid, like the last time he was behind the wheel of a car, and destroyed the lives of the people who now most depended upon him?

He hadn't even had a chance to tell Erin the truth out on the boat today, as he'd planned. Not that it mattered now, he warned himself as the reminder of the envelope he'd found in the office came flooding back. It hardened his resolve. By doing what she'd done, she'd effectively been denying his right to discover if Riley was his baby. He'd have it out with her in his own good time but right now, his son depended upon him and he was going to prove to himself, if to no one else, he was all the father Riley needed.

Relief flooded through every taut muscle in Sam's

body as he eased the car into a space at the after-hours clinic. Erin was already lifting Riley from his car seat. He'd started screaming again as they driven through the winding hills and not even Erin had been able to calm him. She slung her bag over one arm and clutched the baby to her.

"Can you bring his diaper bag for me?" she asked, already heading for the entry.

"Sure," he said to her retreating back.

She was through the door before he'd locked the car. He leaned for a moment against the door, the diaper bag in one hand, car keys in the other. He'd done it. He'd actually conquered his worst fear, and he'd done it for Riley. He took a steadying breath and started to walk toward reception, feeling inordinately proud of what he'd achieved.

Erin and Riley were nowhere to be seen when he entered the reception room. In fact, the waiting area was surprisingly quiet with only one other person on the visitors' seats, slumped in a chair with a year's old, well-thumbed magazine on his lap.

"Can I help you?" the perky young woman behind the desk enquired as he approached.

"I'm with Erin Connell and her baby, Riley?"

"Poor little thing. Yes, one of our doctors could see her right away."

"Can I go through?"

"Oh, you're the father? That's excellent. I didn't get all the details I need from Mrs. Connell. Perhaps you could complete them for me, and sign the consent form relating to Riley's care?"

"Oh, I—" Sam cut himself short.

He was about to say he didn't have the authority to sign on Erin's behalf. But he did. He had every right.

He was Riley Connell's father whether Erin liked it or not and as such he silently picked up the pen from the counter and began to complete the remaining details that were required. He'd just finished them and pushed the clipboard back toward the receptionist when his cellphone rang in his pocket.

The receptionist pointed at a sign on the wall requesting that all mobile devices be switched off or turned to silent. Giving her a nod he reached for the phone, ready to turn it off. Then he saw who was calling him.

His private investigator. He hadn't heard from the guy since he'd told Sam where to find Erin and Riley. Sam had all but given up on him finding any further information. He had to take this call. He had to know what else she might be hiding. Especially in light of what Erin had done by keeping the news about James Connell's DNA test secret.

He accepted the call and headed back out the door, standing just outside in the porch.

"Sam Thornton," he answered.

"Mr. Thornton, I'm glad I could get hold of you. I hope I'm not calling at an inconvenient time."

Sam fielded a strange look from a couple who were walking into the clinic, the woman staring pointedly at the diaper bag still in his hand, the man with her clutching an ice pack to his wrist.

"It's fine," Sam said, stepping out of the porch and into the car park. "Go ahead."

"I've been able to gather some more information about Erin Connell. Information that I think might come in useful for you should you prove to be the baby's father and wish to apply for part or full custody."

Full custody? He hadn't even considered that as an option. Yet. "What sort of information," he demanded, his voice cold. Right now he doubted anything he heard about Erin would surprise him.

"It seems she has a bit of a checkered past. She was a runaway. Her mother reported her as a missing person when Erin was about sixteen. Social Services found her and took her home, but she kept running away. When her mother died in a domestic violence incident Erin slipped through the cracks. No one to keep looking for her, I guess."

Was that why she was so determined to create a perfect home now, Sam wondered privately. "Carry on, there's obviously more," he instructed the investigator.

"Oh, yeah, there's certainly more. There are several records of her being arrested for petty crime—shoplifting, vagrancy and some willful damage."

Sam felt a chill grow in his chest. Who was this person the investigator was talking about? She sounded nothing like the Erin Connell he'd thought he'd come to know. The woman he'd actually, stupidly it now seemed, begun to develop feelings for. He'd been prepared to have it out with her. To confront her about the DNA findings and to share the findings of the latest tests. But now he wasn't so sure. What kind of agenda had she had? Could he even trust her with the truth?

He was reminded of the reason he was here at the clinic in the first place and had the sudden urge to be there with Riley, to ensure that he was getting the best care possible, whatever the cost.

"Look, can I call you back tomorrow?" Sam asked.

"Sure, but there are a couple more things. Did you know the property she's living in now is held in trust?"

"In trust?" She hadn't said anything about that.

"Yeah. Her husband's great-grand-something set it up so that the property can only be used by a direct descendant, by blood. Basically, it means she won't have a roof over her head if you're proven to be the baby's father."

"It's been proven," he answered succinctly, his mind turning over this new piece of information carefully. He'd struggled to understand Erin's reasons for not wanting the DNA tests to be done, but now they were eminently clear. She stood to lose everything and was possibly even prepared to indulge in fraud to ensure that didn't happen. At his expense. Given what he'd learned about her just now, it all began to fit—and the anger he'd been fighting to keep under control flared to scorching life again.

"I guess congratulations are in order then, Mr. Thornton."

"Thanks," Sam said curtly, now more than ever needing to get inside the medical center to see Riley and Erin.

"Before you hang up—" the investigator interjected "—there's more you ought to know."

"Carry on," Sam said, impatience making his words brisk.

"Erin Connell, or rather, Johnson, as she was known then, was once held for questioning in relation to an infant death."

Twelve

All the blood rushed out of Sam's head and went straight to his feet. He dropped the diaper bag and leaned against a nearby signpost.

"She what?" he finally managed to grind out.

"Seems she was living in a squat house. A child died and everyone there closed ranks. Wouldn't divulge any information about the baby's death, which made everyone a suspect. The death wasn't an accident, but no charges were brought, and as far as I'm aware the case is still open."

"When exactly did this happen?" Sam managed to ask even as other questions swirled around in his mind.

"About ten years ago, just before she headed out to Lake Tahoe."

Where she'd subsequently inveigled her way into the heart and the bed of the owner of Connell Lodge, Sam realized. Had she been as cold-blooded as all that? It was possible, especially if she was the kind of woman who could stand by when a child was murdered and agree not see the perpetrator brought to justice. Who did that? And, more important, where did that leave Riley in terms of safety?

Even as he thought that, his mind argued back in kind. He'd seen Erin with Riley, seen how distressed she'd become when he was ill. She was a good mother—fiercely protective and nurturing. He couldn't deny that. But as a person? As a woman who had willfully withheld the truth about all manner of things, she left a great deal to be desired.

"Can you email your findings to me in a report by morning?"

"It's on its way already," the investigator confirmed.

"Great, and thanks."

"It's what you pay me to do, Mr. Thornton."

Sam severed the connection and thought that yeah, that was exactly what he'd paid the investigator to do. He'd had no idea of the scope of what the man would uncover, though. He shook his head slightly. He'd come so close to admitting his feelings to Erin today. What a damned lucky escape that he hadn't. What he knew about her now changed everything as far as he was concerned.

Maybe she'd changed from the runaway who'd turned to petty crime to survive, and maybe she hadn't. Sam really couldn't know for sure. But nothing could excuse what she'd done as recently as two weeks ago in hiding the DNA test results proving her late husband wasn't Riley's father. As far as Sam was concerned, some things were not negotiable and being truthful was one of them. Especially over something as vitally important as the paternity of her son.

He slid his phone back into his pocket and returned to the reception area of the clinic, just in time it seemed. Erin and a far more subdued Riley were coming through from the treatment rooms.

"Everything okay?" he asked, stepping forward and running a hand over Riley's head. He was cooler at least.

"Yeah, he has an ear and throat infection, poor baby. Must have picked something up when we were in town the other day. They've managed to get him to take something to bring his temperature down a little and I need to fill a prescription for a round of antibiotics." She looked over to the receptionist. "I understand I need to complete some more paperwork before we can go?"

The woman smiled back at her. "Oh, no, your husband completed everything for us. If you can just settle the account you'll be good to go."

"I'll take care of that," Sam said, whipping out his wallet and sliding a credit card across the counter.

"Thank you," Erin whispered. "But where did she get the idea that you're my husband?"

"Later," he said succinctly. "Let's get that prescription then get Riley home and settled first."

He swiped up the receipt from the counter and guided Erin back to the car. While she settled Riley in his car seat, Sam went to the pharmacy attached to the clinic and had the prescription filled. As he walked back to the car Erin straightened from where she'd been leaning in through the back door. She looked directly into Sam's eyes as he approached. Could she see in them that he knew the truth about her, he wondered. He'd never been a particularly adept poker player, bluffing just wasn't a part of who he was.

"Would you like me to drive us back?" Erin asked as she accepted the pharmacy bag from Sam.

"Will Riley be okay without you next to him?"

"Good point. The descent on the hill might set him off again. Are you sure you'll be okay, though?"

"I'll take it easy. If there's a problem I'll let you know."

Without waiting for her response he sat at the wheel and waited for her to get in back and buckle her seat belt. The old tension caught in his gut as he started the car and backed out of the parking space, then headed out onto the road. He fought against it. He had overcome this already once today. He could beat this thing, the fear, the sense that he and he alone was responsible for the safe carriage of the one he loved.

When they pulled in at the lodge he was shattered. The concentration it had required to keep his cool while driving back had been monumental, but on top of the weariness he was aware of a sense of achievement. He'd conquered one beast, now all he needed to do was gear up for his next battle.

Riley was grumbling again when Erin pulled him from his car seat and carried him inside.

"I'll get him settled and then I'll get a meal sorted for us," she said, going through to her rooms.

"Sure," Sam said, welcoming the opportunity to get his thoughts together and to decide on the best way to approach this thing.

He went upstairs and stripped off his clothes. It was as if they reeked of the fear that had gripped him when Erin had expected him to drive. He took a quick shower and dressed in a clean pair of jeans and sweater, then made his way back downstairs.

Erin looked up from the casserole she'd obviously retrieved from the freezer.

"Some day, huh?" She put the dish in the microwave, closing the door and punching the necessary buttons.

"Indeed. Is Riley all settled?"

The words felt like cotton wool in his mouth—bulky, difficult to talk around, yet totally lacking in substance.

"Yeah, I slipped his dose of antibiotics into his mouth while nursing him. With that and the painkiller they gave him at the clinic I think he should be much better by morning. At least I hope so."

"Good."

He felt awkward, not an emotion he was used to experiencing. He took a deep breath and searched for the way he wanted to lead the next few minutes. He was forestalled, however, by Erin coming across the kitchen and sliding her hands around his waist to nuzzle against his chest. He raised one hand uncomfortably to her back. Despite all they'd shared earlier today, right now she felt completely foreign to him.

"Thank you for everything today. Especially for driving to the clinic and home again. I know how much that must have cost you, how difficult it must have been for you to drive."

He must have made some sound of assent because she hugged him tight before continuing.

"I hope it wasn't illegal for you to do what you did at the clinic, though. You really shouldn't have signed those papers."

Icy cold water trickled through his veins and Sam slowly and deliberately pulled her arms away from holding him. He took a step back. This was it. This was where he told her the truth. The truth they could have all known sooner if she hadn't been so busy dodging her responsibilities by hedging around the requests for Riley's DNA. The anger that flooded him now was chilling, rather than hot. It seeped through him, penetrating his heart and hardening him against the look of confusion in her eyes as he dropped her arms and shoved his hands in the pockets of his jeans.

"I broke no laws."

"Are you sure? You're not Riley's parent or guardian."

"That's where you're wrong," he said determinedly. "I am Riley's father. I am Party A."

Erin felt the air rush out of her lungs as his words slowly penetrated. *Sam* was Party A? She reached for the back of a kitchen chair, desperate to steady herself and to fight back the swimming black spots that suddenly clouded her vision.

"N-no, that can't be true," she cried, slowly sinking to her knees.

Sam watched her with eyes totally devoid of expression. Devoid of every ounce of the care or compassion or, she'd dared to hope, love, that she'd seen in them earlier today.

"Believe it. I found out this morning. I was going to tell you when we were out on the boat today. I—" His voice broke off and he made a sound of disgust deep in his throat. "I was stupid enough to think we could possibly work toward a future together. The three of us. But that was before I found out that you've known for weeks that James Connell wasn't Riley's father. Why didn't you tell the truth? You had no right to withhold that information."

He was furious, she could see it now in every line of his body, in the tight way he held his mouth, in the lines that had reappeared on his face. She dragged herself back up to her feet.

"I don't believe you! You're lying to me. Where's your proof?" she protested. "Riley is *my* son. Mine! I have a duty to protect him, to protect what's his."

"But this," Sam spread his arms out wide, "isn't his, is it? If James Connell wasn't Riley's father, which we both know he wasn't, then you're also defrauding the trustees of the Connell Estate by continuing to let them think he was."

"How did you—" She stopped herself and took in a shuddering breath. "That's none of your business. I want you to get out of here. I don't want you here anymore!"

Tears were streaming down her cheeks now. Hot angry tears born out of a terror that threatened to grip her tight and never let her go.

"You know you're living here illegally, living here on borrowed time. How could you not want to give him a chance to know his real father?" Sam pressed on, each word a blow to her fragile stability.

She bit down on her lip. She wouldn't answer him. She couldn't. He would never understand that this was her *home,* her sanctuary. It was the one place in her life she'd known stability and safety—where she'd belonged. But she'd been found out—she didn't belong here, and neither did Riley. She knew she didn't have a leg to stand on. She'd been futilely grabbing at straws, hoping that the truth wouldn't come out.

"What? No answers? Why doesn't that surprise me?" His voice dripped with loathing, a far cry from the man with whom she'd made such exquisite love only hours ago. "I'll go in the morning but you can expect to hear from me through my lawyers later tomorrow."

He turned to leave the room, hesitating a moment

in the doorway before turning back to face her. Erin pulled herself up straight, bracing herself for the next blow that she instinctively knew would come.

"You know, I'd been prepared all along to consider joint custody of our son—something you seemed determined to deny me the right to. But you can forget that now. All bets are off."

"How dare you say that," she cried at his retreating back. "No court in the world would give you full custody of a child. You killed your wife, didn't you? You admit yourself your work habits led to your accident. How can you consider yourself a fit parent for sole guardianship when you couldn't be there for your wife? Do you expect a court to believe you'll be there for a baby?"

Sam turned to face her again. This time the expression on his face showed the emotion he'd evidently been holding back. She flinched as he started to speak, his words like spears flying straight toward her.

"Be very careful before casting stones in my direction, Erin Connell. I know about your past—the running away, the shoplifting—*everything*."

In that split second she knew he had somehow become privy to her worst secret and her worst nightmare.

"H-how?"

"How doesn't matter. And I won't stop there, Erin. Before I'm finished I will have unearthed every single last thing there is to know about you, now and from the past. Things that will show you in a very bad light when it comes to considering *your* fitness to be a parent. I think—" he gave her a grim smile "—that by comparison, my work ethic will be the least of my problems."

Thirteen

The microwave let out a long beep, signaling it had completed its task but Erin was oblivious. She sank into one of the kitchen chairs, her whole body shaking with the enormity of what had just happened.

Sam's threats shook her to the core, but as she sat shivering in the chair, her mind was filled with painful images of her life before she came to Lake Tahoe. Her past was dark and murky. She thought she'd put all that behind her, that by being a good employee, a solid citizen and then subsequently a good wife and mother, that she'd paid her dues. But now the memories of the horror and shame of her past filled her again.

The death of the baby in the house she'd lived in had been horrifying on its own. Being publicly vilified when she was accused of conspiring to conceal information about the death had been her worst nightmare.

She hadn't even been home the night the little girl

had been injured and died. After a night of drinking heavily, she'd passed out in an alley and woken in the morning only when a street sweeper had come by. When she got back to the house, the police were there. She'd arrived just in time to be taken into the station for questioning.

The press had been there, the air filled with shouts and the flash and click of cameras. She'd been confused and disoriented—and scared. Very, very scared.

She hadn't willingly conspired with the others in the house, but she had been threatened, and threatened very convincingly, with what might happen if she told the police what she thought had happened. It was no excuse, sure, for not telling the truth, but as she'd told herself at the time, who would have believed her anyway? She was just another runaway. Someone living off the streets, surviving on cunning and luck to get food in her belly each day. Still, the guilt over her silence had haunted her, wrecking the tiny bit of peace of mind she'd found since leaving her mother's house.

It had become her turning point. The line in the sand where she knew she had one chance, and one chance only to make her life right again, to get onto a solid path for a worthy existence. She'd headed for Lake Tahoe, knowing she needed to get away. At the hostel where she'd stayed, she'd found the advertisement for work at Connell Lodge…and the rest was history.

Or rather, the rest *had been* history. Now, if Sam was to be believed, it would all be exposed again. She knew that if any of what had happened at that time was dragged before a Family Court it couldn't help but color how they might deal with her. Especially in light of whom she was up against. Sam's corporate image was world-renowned. The man himself was charismatic, warm and attentive. She'd struck a low blow when she'd dragged his responsibility for his wife's death into the argument. He'd clearly been punishing himself all this time, but any court would see that he was a good man who'd make a wonderful father. His lawyers would see to that.

And all that aside, even if she could fight Sam, even if he had to provide court-ordered maintenance toward Riley's care, she couldn't afford a legal battle. She didn't have two pennies to rub together herself. Everything she and James had built up here at Connell Lodge had been invested back into it. Into the estate that was supposed to form a part of Riley's heritage. A heritage that would now, in accordance with the original James Connell's wishes, be gifted to the State of California.

She had nothing. Nothing and nowhere to go. No job, no prospects. No future.

When the lodge was taken away from her, it would be the tipping point that would see Riley into Sam's care, she just knew it. Every instinct in her screamed at her to run. To pack the car full of every basic item she and Riley could need, to grab him from his crib and to drive until she could find somewhere that Sam Thornton couldn't find her. But in her heart she knew she couldn't do that. It wouldn't be fair to Riley.

So where did that leave her?

If Sam truly was Riley's father then, yes, he did have rights to his son. But until she had categorical proof of those rights and a court order to hand him over, she would not let her baby out of her sight. And, until that moment, Sam Thornton could take a hike.

Wearily she tipped the casserole into the trash. She had no appetite. Once she'd cleaned up the minimal disorder of her kitchen she went through to her room, showered and dressed in her nightgown, only to stare at the dark ceiling all night as sleep eluded her and the terrifying prospect of losing her child filled her mind.

She was still groggy from lack of sleep the next morning. Thankfully, she'd drifted off somewhere around three in the morning, but Riley was an early riser and today was no exception. Her relief was palpable when she went in to get him from his crib. His temperature was back to normal and he was back to his happy gummy-smiling self.

Erin lost herself in the routine of morning, trying desperately not to think about what was going to happen next. By the time she made her way through to the kitchen with Riley she was almost starting to feel normal, despite the hunk of anxiety that sat somewhere between her chest and her stomach. She hadn't been in the kitchen long when she heard Sam enter the room.

"My car will be here shortly," he said bluntly.

She turned slowly, forcing herself to meet his gaze, but she needn't have worried. Sam's attention was one hundred percent on the little boy in the tabletop rocker. Riley crowed and kicked his feet as he saw Sam.

"Good morning, my boy," Sam said, a note of something in his voice Erin couldn't quite put her finger on.

Hunger? Longing? Maybe even love? In an instant she saw the resemblance between the two of them. The square shape of Riley's jaw, the slight indentation that would no doubt, with time, become like the dimple on Sam's chin, as well. Her heart squeezed painfully tight. Now that she knew, she saw other resemblances, too. How could she not have noticed them before? How could she not have questioned Sam's arrival, her first guest inquiry in months, hard on the heels of the letter from the clinic's representatives and the lawyers acting for Party A—Sam? She still found it hard to get her head around the fact that they were one and the same. That he'd deceived her from the very start. The knowledge sent a buzz of anger vibrating through her.

"Feel free to wait outside," she said as curtly as possible and turned back to the baby cereal she'd started Riley on the past few mornings.

"Yeah, I bet you'd like that. But it's not about what you want anymore, Erin. It never was. It's about my son and me."

Erin felt his words as if each one was a physical blow. A solid and hurtful reminder that she wasn't good enough. She'd never been good enough. It was why she'd worked so damn hard to carve out a life for herself here. Away from the father who'd abandoned her as an infant, away from the mother who had taken every opportunity to tell Erin how her very existence had blighted her mother's life. Away from every other person who had let her down, told her she was a failure, that she was no good.

But she'd proven she was better than they'd all said. She'd pulled herself from the brink of what was surely about to become a desperate spiral. She'd become reliable, focused, strong. She pulled her shoulders back and faced Sam as calmly as she could.

"Thank you for your honesty. It's probably one of the few truths you've delivered to me the whole time you've been here. Now, if you'll excuse Riley and me, we're going to my private quarters to eat our breakfast. Please pull the front door closed behind you on your way out.

She leaned across the table and deftly unclipped Riley from his rocker. Holding him to her, she gathered his breakfast cereal and went through to her sitting room, closing the door behind her and locking it for good measure. She waited on the other side of the door, listening for Sam's movement. He must have stood there on the other side for some time but eventually she heard his uneven gait as he left the room. It was a small victory, but right now she'd take whatever she could get.

It was later in the morning that Sasha came around, to share a coffee and to check up on Riley. She was thrilled to see him feeling so much better so quickly. She was less so about Erin's news about Sam.

"He's Riley's father?" Sasha's eyebrows almost shot into her hairline.

"So he says. I won't accept it until I have proof, though. Legal proof."

"I wouldn't either. Except…"

"Except what?" Erin demanded, her nerves frayed.

"Except I kept thinking there was something familiar about Sam Thornton from the first time I met him. It was his similarities to Riley. They really do look alike."

Erin sighed and felt her entire body sag. So Sasha had noticed it, too. She really didn't stand a chance and said as much to her friend.

"Don't be silly. You're still Riley's mother."

"But he's going to go for full custody and, Sash, I'm frightened he'll get it. I…I've done things in my past that I'm deeply ashamed of. He knows all of it and he's not above using it to prove he is a far more worthy parent. With his money he can afford the best lawyers, the best advice, the best of everything. I can't."

Sasha reached across the table and gripped Erin's hand tight. "Don't borrow trouble. Let's wait and see what he comes up with first. If need be Tony and I can loan you money to fight this."

Tears pooled in Erin's eyes as she squeezed Sasha's

hand right back. Words failed her in the face of her friend's staunch support.

"And we'll be character witnesses, too. We were James's friends for years, we've known you from the moment you arrived here. We *know* you, Erin. We know the person you are now and the amazing mother you've become. It's got to count for something, right?"

She could only hope.

The day stretched out before her once Sasha left. Erin remembered she needed to clean up the boat and get it ready before the dry stack guys came to collect it later in the week. Had it really only been a day since she and Sam had motored out of the cove? Memories of that day were some of the best of her life—and some of the worst.

She bundled Riley up in warm clothes and put him in his stroller, throwing her supplies in a large shopping bag. Sam must have affixed the gangway from the boat to the dock yesterday before disembarking. If she wasn't still so furious with him she'd have mentally thanked him for the consideration. She pushed Riley's stroller onto the boat without any difficulty and tucked him in a sunny corner out of the wind, where he promptly dozed off.

Local birds had made short work of the leftovers on the table, leaving their own very personal form of thanks on the crockery. Erin mechanically went through the motions of tidying everything up and bagging what needed to go into the trash before scrubbing the tabletop down with disinfectant and hot water. Once the exterior was spick-and-span, she knew she couldn't avoid going into the cabin.

"Time to put my big girl panties on, Riley," she said to her slumbering child as she went down the steps.

The bed was exactly as they'd left it, sheets a-tumble, covers strewn to the floor. A sharp spear of pain lanced through her as she reached forward to rip the sheets from the bed. Yesterday had held so much promise. So much hope. So much love. And now it was nothing but a tangled memory. She roughly bundled the sheets into a ball, shoving them into a laundry bag and breathing through her mouth so she wouldn't catch so much as a whiff of Sam's cologne.

She also packed up the coverlet and the pillows. They could all do with dry cleaning before getting put into storage for next season. She shook her head. Why was she even worrying about next season? There was no point. She would be leaving Connell Lodge soon.

She wondered if she had an out somehow. If there wasn't some legal loophole she could utilize. Erin reminded herself to contact Janet Morin and ask her if she could study the terms of her right to reside at the lodge, not to mention the latest situation with Sam.

Back at the house, Riley transferred easily from his stroller and into his bed. The antibiotics seemed to make him sleepier than normal, she thought, but that in itself was a relief. She knew sleep was a great healer and she could already see a major improvement in his well-being. It was selfish of her to wish he was more wakeful just so she'd have some company and wouldn't have to be alone with the thoughts tumbling after one another in her mind.

She decided she'd go up to Sam's room and quickly clean out the last remnants of his occupancy, then she'd give Janet a call. Flinging open the bedroom window to air the room out, she methodically stripped the bed and removed the towels and robe from the bathroom. Then she cleaned until she thought her hands would bleed from the effort. Finally satisfied she'd scoured away every last remnant of Sam's stay at Connell Lodge, Erin closed the window and went back downstairs.

There was no avoiding it any longer. She needed to talk to Janet. She half smiled. Her habit of avoidance was getting to be a little too much of a regular occurrence. Luckily, Janet was free when Erin phoned.

"I'm glad you called," the lawyer said. "I was going to get in touch with you today."

"The news about Sam Thornton being Party A?" Erin replied. "I already know."

"No, not that. Really? Your guest is Riley's father?" Janet's shock was clear through the line.

"Apparently. I believe his lawyers will be sending proof sometime today."

"Wow, how do you feel about that?"

"Threatened."

She dragged in a deep breath and explained the situation, ending with what Sam had accused her of in regard to lying to stay in the house.

"So, is there any way we can challenge the terms of the trust?" she finished.

"That's a tough question. I'll do what I can to find out. I have a colleague with another firm who'd probably love to get his hands on this. He's a bit of an expert."

"Expensive?"

"He owes me a favor, don't worry about fees."

Erin heaved a small sigh of relief then remembered that Janet had wanted to talk to her, too. "What was it you wanted to call me about?"

"Let's see, ah, yes, here it is. It seems there was some anomaly with your DNA test. They want you to test again. They've sent the requirements here to my office.

If you can make it in this afternoon, I can get them out on the late courier in the evening."

Erin had found it strange that she'd been requested to supply a DNA sample at the same time as Riley's. Janet had assured her it had to do with providing a complete profile for Riley's parentage and after that Erin hadn't given it another thought. She shot a look at the clock. She could make the trip when Riley woke from his nap and said as much to Janet.

"Good, I'll look forward to seeing you soon."

She hung up from the call, trepidation seeping through her body. The world that had been her rock, her bastion of security, was crumbling around her, piece by painful piece. And as much as she appreciated the support she'd received from friends like Sasha and Janet, she couldn't help but fear that the damage wasn't over yet.

Fourteen

Sam paced the floor in David Fox's office.

"You're going to wear a hole in the carpet if you keep that up," David said with a droll smile on his face.

"For what I'm paying you, you can afford to replace it," he snapped in return.

He caught the look on David's face and felt ashamed. His lawyer wasn't the reason for his bad temper. This new development was.

"You know this means you have a stronger case, don't you? Riley is not only your baby, he's Laura's, too."

It was beyond belief. Sam closed his eyes as he let the words soak in once more. How could such a mistake have been made?

"So there's no doubt? Erin is not Riley's biological mother?"

"No doubt at all." David leaned forward and lifted a

sheaf of papers from his desk. "There's been some further investigation into the leak about the mistake at the clinic. It seems that Mrs. Connell was implanted with the wrong embryo. When you and Laura didn't arrive for your appointment someone slipped up big-time."

Sam threw himself into one of David's visitor chairs and reached up a hand to pinch the bridge of his nose. He couldn't believe what he'd just heard. It had been enough to know that Riley was his son, but to discover that he was Laura's as well was a gift he didn't deserve. But *she* did, he reminded himself. Laura had wanted nothing more than to be a mother. He could ensure that Riley grew up knowing what a wonderful and special person she was.

"What a mess," he muttered, lost for any better description.

"Seems cut-and-dried to me."

"What about Erin? Does she know yet?"

"We sent the information through her lawyer so I believe she will have been apprised of the situation by now."

"She'll be devastated."

"Not your problem," David said succinctly.

"Have a heart," Sam protested. "I know she did her best to block our attempts to find out if I was Riley's father, but we have to see her side, too."

"Why the turnaround? Just ten days you were so angry I thought you were going to ask me to stage an abduction to get Riley out of her evil clutches."

Sam rose from the chair and began to pace anew. "I know," he admitted wryly. "But I've had time to cool down. To think. She loves him so much. That's why she fought so hard to block us. I hate to admit it, but if the situation was reversed I probably would've done the same."

"Do you want to revise your bid for full custody?" David sounded confused.

Not his lawyer's natural state, Sam noted to himself, but nothing about this situation was natural or clear-cut any more.

"Absolutely not," he said emphatically. That was the one thing he was certain of. Now even more so. "But perhaps we can offer her visitation. She bore him, after all. She's nursed him and raised him for nearly six months. I have to show some compassion."

He held up a hand as David began to speak. Knowing, without hearing it, that the lawyer was going to refute what he'd just said. He knew he didn't have to be fair or reasonable about anything. He had the money and he had the influence to make what he wanted to happen, happen—not to mention, in the eyes of many, the right to raise Riley. But since he'd left Lake Tahoe he hadn't been able to get Erin out of his mind.

"And a settlement. A generous one. I don't want her on the street because of all this. She's as much a victim as I am."

"Have you sustained a knock to the head or something, Sam?" David asked, then after receiving a stony look from his client he just shook his head. "I know, I know. You're the client, you call the shots. Well, if you're one hundred percent certain that's what you want me to do, I'll do it. You know, the issue with Erin Connell is cloudy, but she may still have some rights as Riley's surrogate mother. Rights she hasn't legally signed away—yet. Perhaps we can forestall any pitfalls here by acknowledging and defining those potential rights immediately. I'll draw up the papers in the next few days and we can go over them. What sort of settlement amount were you thinking?"

His eyebrows rose when Sam named the sum he wanted.

"You really are serious, aren't you?" David said, his voice somewhat awestruck.

"I've never been more serious in my life. Call me when you have the details ironed out."

Sam turned on his handcrafted leather heel and walked out of David's office trying to ignore the feeling that he still hadn't done quite enough. But he had. He had done everything in his power to do the right thing by his son. And Erin wouldn't miss out. With the settlement he had proposed she'd have more than enough money to buy a new home, and if she wanted to, attempt IVF again for another child. It was the best he could do, he told himself resolutely.

Erin tossed the mail she'd cleared from her post office box in town on the kitchen table. She knew she should have been in earlier, but lately she'd barely been able to bring herself to leave the house. When she'd stopped answering her phone, Sasha had made a point to come over each day, to check up on her, and she'd appreciated it, but she'd wanted some space to herself, too. Space in which to grieve, not just for the loss of the relationship she'd hoped to share with Sam, but for her home, her life—nearly everything she held dear.

Riley had fallen asleep in his carrier and she'd managed to transfer him to his crib without his waking. Sometimes she forgot to count her blessings. Through all this time, he'd been an absolute angel. At least she had him. She'd find some way to fight Sam's bid for full custody—she just had to. It was going to be a tough road, especially since the trustees had given her notice to quit the property so it could be prepared to be gifted to the State.

It felt sometimes as if the blows never stopped falling. When Janet had told her the trust's details regarding descendants's right to reside at the property was watertight she'd known it would be only a matter of time before she and Riley would have to pack up their few personal possessions and leave. She didn't really know what was worse. The years of abuse and neglect she'd endured at her mother's hands, or this.

It had been horrible growing up without any sense of her home as a safe haven, but in many ways it was harder to finally have the home she'd always wanted and then have it taken away from her. Being forced to walk away from her home, her livelihood, everything, was devastating.

Erin flicked on the coffee machine and picked up the envelopes, idly thumbing through them while she waited for the machine to finish. She sorted them into different piles—ones she knew were related to the lodge, personal ones, junk mail. She hesitated over the second-to-last envelope in the stack. The high-quality heavy white envelope with the subtle logo and return address had escaped her notice when she'd collected the mail, but she recognized it instantly now.

Sam's lawyers. Her blood ran cold and she put that envelope to one side, not quite ready yet to read in deliberate black and white, the extent of his threat to her. Maybe she should have returned those calls Janet had been leaving on her answering machine the past few days.

Mechanically she went through the motions of pouring her coffee and taking it to the table, debating whether or not to call Janet now. After all, forewarned was forearmed, right? But some gut instinct told her that no matter what Janet had to say, it wouldn't change what was in that envelope. She'd have to deal with it, one way or another. Erin sat in a chair and turned the large envelope over in her hands. She couldn't put it off any longer. She slid the tip of her little finger under the tiny open bit at the edge of the flap and tore it away until she could slide her whole finger into the gap and rip open the packet.

Carefully, she pulled out a folded sheaf of papers clipped to a covering letter. Her eyes skimmed the letter once, twice, three times. It didn't make sense. It couldn't.

She flicked to the next page, which tabulated laboratory results, twice. Both the first test she'd had done and the second. She shook her head, unable to believe the evidence before her very eyes.

She was not Riley's mother.

"No!" The word slipped from her in a tortured wail as a spasm of pain more intense than anything she had ever endured before knifed through her body.

She wasn't Riley's mother? That was impossible. It couldn't be true. She'd felt the unbelievably sweet flicker of his first movements, carried him to term. She'd nearly lost her life giving birth to him, a birth so full of complications that it was impossible for her to bear another child. She'd nurtured him from the moment she'd been able to. How could she not be his mother? The emptiness she'd felt since learning Sam was Riley's father was nothing compared to the clawing pain that scored her now.

Riley was *her* baby, *her* son—the child of her heart. It wasn't enough that the clinic had made a mistake with the fertilization, but to have made such a disastrous error as to impregnate her with another couple's baby? It was wrong on so many levels she couldn't even begin to grasp them. All she knew was that it hurt, it hurt so badly she wondered if she would ever be able to function properly ever again.

Her coffee had gone stone-cold by the time she summoned the courage to continue to read the papers that had been included in the packet. It appeared the mistake had been deliberate. Further investigation had shown that the incident had been what caused the whistle-blower to come forward. James and Erin's sole viable embryo from their IVF had been accidentally destroyed. The whistle-blower had been instructed to find a replacement embryo for implantation to hide the fact that the mistake had occurred. One of three embryos, readied for another couple due for implantation on the same day, had been implanted instead. That couple had never made it to the clinic because of a car wreck.

Everything now fell into awful place. Sam's guilt over his wife's death, his determination to find out if Riley was his son. She wondered, briefly, if he'd been as shocked as she was over the news that she'd carried his and Laura's child. It was too much to take in, all of it.

Hot tears spilled from her eyes and tracked down her cheeks. Tremors began to rack her body, at first small and then bigger and bigger until she began to sob out loud. Harsh wrenching sobs that filled the room with her anguish, an anguish she knew nothing could ever assuage.

When reality began to set in, Erin knew deep in her heart that there was no way, now, that Sam's petition to have full custody of Riley could be unsuccessful. No way on earth. And how could she, in all honesty, contest his right to his son, the child who'd resulted from his DNA and his wife's? It would be contesting Riley's right to his real father, a man she already knew, first-hand, loved the little boy. She'd seen it in his eyes, in his actions, in every moment he'd been able to share with Riley during his time at the lodge.

But she'd borne Riley, she was the only mother he knew and he depended on her.

Nothing and no one is irreplaceable. The words echoed in her mind as if James were in the room with her now. It was something he'd always said whenever they'd lost a valued staff member. And he'd been right. Even as her heart argued that this was different—she was Riley's *mother,* for goodness' sake!—her head knew that on paper it made little difference. She'd been a surrogate. She'd given birth to another couple's child.

It was unbearable. It was a mistake that should never, ever have been made. She'd thought her life couldn't sink any lower, that things couldn't possibly get worse, but she'd been so very wrong. Through vision blurred with the tears that continued to fall, she looked through the balance of the papers, identifying a visitation document and another one entitled Settlement Agreement.

A settlement? What on earth? She flicked through the papers and began to feel her grief become sharper, even more agonizing, as it blended with pure fury when she saw the terms that Sam was proposing. In a nutshell, he wanted to pay her a million dollars, in full and final payment and in gratitude for carrying his son and pro-viding for him in the first six months of his life. Pro-vision was being made to give her time to wean Riley onto formula before he was handed over to his father.

One word leaped from the page, searing itself against the back of her eyes. *Gratitude?* Erin clenched her jaw and swallowed hard. He was *grateful* she'd given him a son to take home and love and raise? How dare he reduce her arduous, joyful, life-changing months of motherhood to nothing more than a service provided by a paid employee? She carefully put the papers down on the table, fighting the urge to rip them into shreds.

A million dollars? Is that what Sam thought a child was worth? He was *paying* her for his son? No. No way. How dare he? How could he put a price on a life? On what she'd gone through? On what she was losing— what he was taking from her?

She pushed herself up to her feet so rapidly her chair fell, bouncing on the tiled floor. Grabbing the cordless phone she dialed Janet's number, feeling as if she was holding on to her sanity by no more than a thread.

Janet wasn't available but Erin was able to make an appointment to see her the next day. When she hung up, she sat down again and read every paper through, over and over, until she felt she understood every last word.

She couldn't fight his claim for full custody but she could hold some power here. It was the only power she had left.

Fifteen

"What do you mean she won't accept the money? Why? Isn't it enough? Is she asking for more?" Sam raged through his phone.

"I mean, she won't accept the money. *Any* money."

David's cool clear voice sounded absurdly rational in light of the information he'd just disclosed.

"She has to."

The words sounded about as lame and redundant as Sam felt right now.

"Actually, no. She doesn't. Her only request is for an extra two weeks for weaning the child."

"Riley. His name is Riley."

"But you'll be changing that, right? Didn't you and Laura have a different name picked out?"

Sam squeezed the phone so tight the plastic squeaked. "No, I won't be changing his name. And I am going to do my best to change Erin's mind about the money."

"Well, good luck on that, Sam. From what her lawyer has said, she's pretty adamant."

Sam ended the call and paced the confines of his high-rise office overlooking Union Square. The question "why?" echoed back and forth in his head. She'd made no counteroffer on the custody bid, she'd ignored the visitation rights and she'd refused the settlement. What the hell was going on? He, probably better than most, knew she couldn't *afford* to refuse the money.

He stopped in front of the window, staring down at the people rushing about their busy lives out on the street, on the beggars and homeless people who dotted the pavement here and there. Would any one of them refuse an offer of a million dollars? No, of course not. No rational person would.

He had to see her. To talk to her. To talk some sense into her. He knew her background. He'd read the report from the investigator. She'd grown up with little more than ill-fitting clothing and the bruises on her back. Subsequent to that had come a history of running away from home, substance abuse and the list of petty crimes she'd been picked up for.

After the baby from the squat house died, she'd made a conscious and massive effort to distance herself from her past and to clean herself up. To improve her life and to build a new one filled with all that she'd had a right to before, but had never been given.

Sam had read the report and been drowned in shame. He'd been prepared to tar her with the same brush as the police officers who'd investigated the infant's death. But they hadn't known her. *He* did. Anger and heartbreak had blinded him when they'd fought after bringing Riley home from the emergency doctor, but once that anger had cooled, he'd had to admit that she truly was the kind, capable, loving woman he'd come to know over the past few months.

He finally understood why she'd been so determined to hold on to it all. Been prepared to lie about Riley's paternity to keep their home. He'd gone through the wringer the past few weeks, and his early anger had settled down to a slow burn, but all that was nothing compared to what he knew she must be feeling now. He made a decision. He was going to Connell Cove and he wasn't coming back until Erin agreed to allow him to ensure that she was financially secure.

He crossed back to his desk and picked up his phone to talk to his executive assistant.

"Julia, get me on the next flight to Lake Tahoe, I don't care which airport, just whichever one leaves soonest. If there are no commercial flights then charter one. And make sure there's a rental car there for me, too."

"A rental car? Did you want a driver?"

"No, I'll be driving myself."

"Are you sure, Sam?"

He ruthlessly quelled the instinctive thrust of fear that pushed from the back of his mind. "Absolutely certain."

"Okay, then."

He waited about ten minutes until she called him back with the details. He didn't even head back to his apartment for a change of clothes, instead getting Ray to take him straight out to the airport. One way or another, he'd settle this with Erin Connell before the night was out.

It had been the week from hell, knowing each time she nursed Riley it was taking her one step closer to the last time, and ultimately, the day she would have to say goodbye to him. For good. She'd ignored the visitation rights that Sam's lawyer had included in the documents. She knew in her heart it was better this way. Better than only seeing Riley for a few short hours every few weeks. Knowing such torture would probably be even more painful than not seeing him at all. She simply couldn't face having to walk away from him each time, knowing someone else was loving him, raising him into boyhood, then manhood. Someone who wasn't her.

She'd put Riley to bed for the night a little while ago. For some reason, tonight it had been hard to actually put him down and walk away, leaving him to settle into slumber. All she'd wanted to do these past days was hold him and never let him go.

Maybe it had been the confirmation from the trustees of the property that the land and house would be signed over to the State on the same date she had agreed to hand over custody of Riley. It was as if every tie to her happiness would be severed at once. She'd considered putting a proposal together to the trustees, to be put forward to whichever organization would be managing the property, appointing her as caretaker. But then she'd changed her mind.

She couldn't bear to think of living the next few years in the place that had seen both the beginning, and the death, of all her dreams. It would be hard to leave here, incredibly hard, because even with the sadness that had been borne out of the past few months, there had been so many good, strong memories. But living here would be so much harder with every second of every day filled with memories of Riley and of what might have been.

Erin was going into the kitchen to make herself

a cup of herbal tea, when she heard a vehicle on the driveway outside. Instead of stopping at the front entrance, it came down the side and pulled up outside the kitchen door. She looked at the clock, and saw that it was nearly eight o'clock. She certainly wasn't expecting anyone this late, but only her friends came round the back like that.

The slam of the car door echoed outside. She strained her ears and heard the uneven, heavy tread of footsteps coming toward the house. Her heart skipped a beat. She only knew one person, one *man,* who walked like that. Sam. Her hand fluttered to her throat.

What was he doing here? Surely he hadn't reneged on the deal giving her the extra weeks with Riley. He was going to have him for the rest of his life, for goodness's sake. What was an extra fourteen days in the scheme of things? Had she missed something in the legal jargon?

Even though she was expecting the knock at the door, Erin jumped when the sharp, decisive sound reverberated through the ancient wood. She forced her legs to move, forced her hand to lift the latch and to swing the door wide. Even though she knew it had to be him, actually seeing him again was a shock. One that sent her heart plummeting to her stomach. She fought to hold on to her self-control, to show him he didn't affect her anymore.

"What do you want?" she demanded.

"Good evening to you, too," Sam said looking steadily into her eyes.

She felt that familiar pull deep in her body, that traitorous draw of attraction that had been so instant, so instinctive, so very, very real. She clamped down on it, immediately. Attraction aside, they shared nothing anymore. Not even the child she'd borne and cherished with every beat of her battered heart.

Her eyes roamed his face, noting the depth of the lines that showed when he was tired or in pain. He was still dressed in a business suit that looked slightly the worse for wear and the length of his journey was evident in his eyes. She tried not to care.

"I'm not taking guests," she said coldly. "You'll have to find somewhere else to stay."

She started to close the door but Sam put his hand up, arresting its progress.

"I'm not here to stay. Please," he said. "We need to talk."

"We've 'talked' all we need to, through our lawyers."

"No, we haven't. Let me in, Erin. If you don't, I'll just stay out here and keep knocking until you do."

The implacable look in his eyes confirmed his intentions. Without saying anything, Erin stepped aside and watched as Sam limped into the kitchen. The place where he'd ripped her world apart only three weeks ago. His limp was more pronounced than usual. She told herself she wasn't concerned for his comfort, even as the words offering him a chair spilled from her mouth.

He lowered himself into a seat, stretching out his injured leg and rubbing it absently. "Is Riley in bed already?"

"Of course." She crossed her arms across her stomach, waiting for the words she dreaded hearing.

"That's a shame. I was hoping I could see him."

"Then perhaps you should have made an appointment through your lawyer."

She couldn't help it, the anger just boiled and boiled inside of her. She held on to it, knowing it was the only thing that was going to get her through this meeting, let alone the next few days, weeks and months. Silence stretched out between them. It seemed they were at a stalemate. Sam looked at her and sighed ever so quietly. She turned away, unable to bear his scrutiny. More anxious now than she'd been before for the calming herbal brew, she busied herself at the kitchen counter.

"I was just making myself a cup of herbal tea. Can I get you anything?" she offered reluctantly.

A look of surprise passed his face. "Sure, a coffee would be great, thanks."

"Decaf or full strength?"

"Better make it full strength."

She moved to the coffeemaker and went through the motions, even as the one big question she really wanted to ask him buzzed around in her head like a particularly angry bee. What the hell was he doing here?

Once she'd made his coffee, exactly the way he liked it, she took it and her tea to the table. She should invite him to sit more comfortably in her sitting room or the library, she thought, but then her anger reasserted itself. It wasn't as if he was an invited guest, after all. Let him sit on a hard wooden kitchen chair.

She sat opposite him, not willing to speak until he spoke first. He took a long draw of his coffee then sighed.

"That's good, thanks."

The silence between them deepened. Erin went to pick up her mug but noticed her hand was shaking. Determined not to show any sign of weakness in front of Sam, she let her hand drop to her lap once more, her fingers now curled into a fist of frustration.

"Why won't you accept the money?" Sam asked bluntly after taking another sip of his coffee. "I know you need it."

"It's not about money."

"What is it then, pride? You can't afford to be proud about this, Erin. I know you're going to lose the roof over your head. Rejecting the settlement is the last thing you need right now."

"What do you care? You'll have what you want."

A look of compassion shone briefly in his eyes before going again so swiftly she began to even wonder if she'd seen it at all.

"You deserve to be compensated. Please, let me do this for you, Erin."

She shook her head. "Compensated? Did I really hear you say that? How dare you. Do you really think you can put a price on your baby's head, Sam? Is that what this is all about?"

"No, of course not!" he protested.

"Then what is it?"

"It's about taking care of you, looking after your best interests."

"That's a pile of crap and you know it. If you had wanted to take care of me you would have been honest with me from the outset. When you arrived here you would have identified yourself instead of making me—"

She cut off before she could lay herself open to even more hurt. There was no way she was going to bare her heart to him, to expose the feelings he'd ridden roughshod over.

"Making you what?" he prompted, leaning forward slightly in his seat.

"No," she shook her head vehemently. "This isn't about me. It's not even about Riley. It's about you trying to ease your guilt—first your guilt about the accident and now the guilt you feel for taking the one thing left to me that has any meaning at all."

She could see she'd struck a blow as his lips firmed into a straight line and his eyes darkened ominously.

"Okay, so if I admit I feel guilty, will you accept the money?"

She laughed, a sharp bitter sound that hung on the air like acrid smoke from a fire.

"I don't believe this. Do all people like you, people with money, think that if you throw enough of it at a problem that it will solve everything? Sam, don't you understand, this offer of yours is an insult."

"What, it's not enough?"

She could hear the beginning of anger in his voice and she welcomed it. It was better than the emotionless, rational man who'd sat at her table the past few minutes.

"It could never be enough."

"Why? Because you can't *buy* a baby? Is that what you think I'm trying to do?"

"You tell me. It sure as hell looks like it. People think they can do it all the time, don't they?" she fired back. "But that's got nothing to do with this, with us. You will have Riley. I signed your papers giving up my rights as his mother."

She closed her eyes and fought for some semblance of control. "Do you have any idea of what that did to me? To just give him away? I didn't enter that pregnancy as a surrogate. I entered it believing the child I carried belonged to me and my husband. Every step of that pregnancy he was ours. Every single step. Riley couldn't be more my son if he *was* my own flesh and blood. I had to do what was best for him. He deserves, more than anyone, a real parent who loves him and who will do the best for him, always. God help you if you ever fail him."

"I won't fail him. If I thought I would, I would never

have worked so hard to get him. I've learned my lesson and I've been lucky to be given a second chance. There is no way on this earth I am going to jeopardize that." He shoved a hand through his hair. "Look, I know you love Riley. I want you to have access to him." Sam's voice was annoyingly reasonable—placating, almost.

"Access!" She virtually spat the word at him. "I don't want access. I wanted to be his mother, to be a full-time part of his life, not just some woman who comes to visit him the occasional weekend. Seeing him only briefly and then having to walk away, time and time again—do you have any idea of how hard that will be for me? How cruel?"

"Are you telling me you don't want to see him?"

"It's what's best, for both of us. What happens if you marry again, when your new wife becomes Riley's mother? Having me around will just confuse things for him."

"I can't believe you're doing this."

"Just leave it, Sam." Erin shook her head emphatically. "I'm not changing my mind."

"I still want you to have the money. It's important to me and before you jam it down my throat again, it's not to assuage my guilt. Nothing will ever lessen my responsibility for what I did, for the choices I made that day. No amount of money could ever repay you for what you've been through. That's why, more than ever, I want you to have it. Name a figure, any figure. It's yours."

Erin shook her head again. He'd never understand.

Sam continued, oblivious to the deepening sorrow in her eyes. The sorrow now consuming the anger that had fired her up only seconds ago. The sorrow that now leeched all the fight out of her.

"Erin, I want you to have the money so you can make

a new home, and maybe have another baby. So if you want to, you can have IVF again and not have to rely on a lottery to do so. This way—"

Wham! And just like that, the anger was back. Buoying her up from the pit she'd been descending to.

"This way, what?" She slammed her hand on the table. "This way you think I can just have another child and that how I feel about Riley, about feeling him grow inside me, about giving birth to him, about caring for him, loving him—that it will all just go away? That I'll *forget* because of something new?"

"No, that's not what I mean." He was raising his voice now, too.

"Keep your filthy money," she sneered. "I don't want any of it."

"But don't you see? Another baby would help."

"No, it wouldn't. Besides, it's impossible."

"Erin, I know it's not as if you've lost a puppy and I'm offering to buy you a new one. I'm not that insensitive. You're a great mother. You deserve this. Let me help you."

Her voice, when she finally managed to speak, was nothing more than a broken whisper. She stared down at her hands knotted together in her lap and squeezed her fingers together tight, as if by doing so she could make some of the pain that surrounded her heart in an unrelenting grip, go away.

"You can't help me."

"Why not? Because you won't let me? I'm sorry, but if your anger with me is what's holding you back then that's just not good enough. Give me one good reason, Erin. One good reason why I can't help you."

She raised her face and made herself meet his eyes. She took a deep breath and expelled it softly.

"Because I can't have any more children. That's why."

Sixteen

Sam sat there, stunned. She couldn't have any more children? Why hadn't that been included in any of the information he'd been given about her? He'd thought he knew it all.

"I'd like you to go now," she said, her voice still husky.

"I'm not going until you tell me everything, Erin. Why can't you have any more children?"

"If I tell you, will you go then?"

Her pain was stark on her face, the wounds she still bore clear in her eyes. He nodded.

"I was overdue and they had to induce me for labor. My doctor had wanted to perform a C-section but I was adamant. We'd had to do everything with artificial help all the way—I wanted to deliver my baby naturally." She cupped her hands around her mug and lifted it to her mouth, taking a long drink of the brew. When she put the mug down she stared at it, as if it was easier to stare at the tea than at him. "Anyway, my labor progressed rather rapidly once they induced me and because of the intensity I accepted pain relief. I'd been given the all-clear to push when I felt it. There was a pain so intense it trumped the epidural. I knew something was very wrong. I told the nurse. Before I knew it, they were wheeling me into an operating room. By then, I was beginning to lose it. I don't remember a whole lot after that except waking up to be told that Riley had been born and was in the neonatal intensive care unit.

"Apparently the pain was caused by my uterus tearing open. When that happened, Riley was deprived of oxygen. Thankfully, they acted fast and he resuscitated without any problems. It could have been a lot worse for him. He was lucky. After four nights in intensive care, he was all clear."

"And you," Sam asked, suddenly desperate to know what had happened to Erin next.

"Me, well, I wasn't so lucky. The uterine rupture had caused too much damage. I had to have a full hysterectomy." She drew in another deep breath and lifted her eyes to his. "So, there you have it. No more babies."

She pushed herself up from the table and walked toward the kitchen door. Her body sagged with the toll it had obviously taken to recount her story. He watched as she opened the door and held it wide.

"You can go now."

He wanted to argue that they weren't finished yet, but he'd already said he would go when she answered his question. He had to honor what he'd promised even though every instinct urged him to stay. The emotional cost of tonight's visit had been high. He wanted, desperately, to make it right for her, but there was nothing he could do and the helplessness of that truth settled in his gut like a heavy weight.

But she couldn't stop him returning, and he would be back. First thing in the morning.

The motel he checked into was nowhere near as comfortable as Connell Lodge, but for the money he didn't expect much. He found a twenty-four-hour convenience store not too far away, where he bought a few toiletries and a budget pack of briefs. He wasn't too sure if the motel provided an overnight laundry service and even if they did he wasn't too sure he'd get his stuff back in time. Nothing was going to delay him tomorrow.

After a quick call to leave a message for Julia, telling his assistant he might be a few days, he went to bed. The night passed slowly as he struggled to find sleep. What Erin had shared with him tonight made her decision to cease her fight to keep Riley even more difficult to come to terms with. He struggled to assimilate that information with what he'd learned from the private investigator.

In treating her as he had, in believing the very worst, and at face value, he'd made a terrible mistake. This all should have turned out so differently. Until he'd discovered that envelope in her office, he'd begun to hope they could possibly spend the rest of their lives together. He could understand why she'd clung so hard to the life she'd fought to create. Was it possible to turn back the clock?

He doubted it. He'd hurt her, and hurt her badly. Why on earth would she trust him again? Based on how he'd treated her, if he were in the same position, he certainly wouldn't. He fought to find a solution, one that would work for all of them. By the time dawn broke through the flimsy bedroom curtains, he was no closer to an answer. All he could do was apologize for what he'd put her through, and then trust she was willing to work from there.

As he negotiated the road down to Connell Cove again he hoped against hope that he could convince her, because somewhere in the lonely hours just gone he'd realized a truth that he hadn't wanted to consider before.

He still loved Erin Connell. No matter her past. No matter how she'd tried to hide the truth about her late husband not being Riley's father. He loved her. It was as simple as that. All he had to do was convince her.

"What now?" Erin said as she opened the door to him again, Riley in her arms.

The instant the little boy saw Sam he opened his arms and babbled a stream of happy baby-speak. Sam's heart swelled with delight—a sensation he welcomed back into his life. Riley wanted him. It was the most incredible feeling in the world. Hard on its heels came an even deeper understanding of what it would be like for Erin, giving Riley up.

Leaving here as he had a few weeks ago had been tough, not knowing how long it would be before he saw Riley again, but the light at the end of the tunnel had been that he'd known he would. That eventually Riley would be his. Now, the thought of walking away and never seeing his son again was enough to pitch his stomach and make him want to fight back and fight hard. How much worse was it for Erin?

Had his threats to her that awful night he'd confronted Erin driven all the fight out of her? Was that why she was no longer fighting for her baby? She'd struck him as the kind of woman who'd be near feral in protecting her child. She'd been prepared to lie to everyone to keep Riley and keep their home. Exactly when had that stopped being so important to her?

"May I?" he asked Erin, waiting for what felt like an eon before she gave a small nod and passed Riley to him.

"I suppose you'd better come in," she said begrudgingly.

"Thank you," he said, hoping he'd infused his words with the genuine thanks he was feeling.

She led him into her sitting room where Riley's play gym was on the floor.

"You can set him down there," she said, pointing to the mat and toys.

Reluctantly, Sam did as she suggested and was pleasantly surprised when he saw Riley roll over from his back to his tummy.

"He can roll over!"

"Yeah, he's been doing it for a few days now. Thinks he's pretty clever."

Sam heard the bittersweet tone in her voice and it drove a stake into his heart. This was one milestone she could still be a part of, but what came next? The enormity of her giving Riley up just hitched another notch. A sudden desperate urge to protect her from any more harm mushroomed inside him. He was the instigator of all of her unhappiness. He had to make it up to her.

"Why are you back?" she asked. "I thought I made my position clear last night."

"You did. But I wanted to apologize to you. For some stupid reason I really did think that throwing money at you would absolve me of some guilt, but I was very wrong. I didn't mean to hurt you more, Erin. When I left here weeks ago, I was so angry I could only see one thing and that was getting Riley. I never stopped to think about what it would do to you, only about what I'd missed out on, what I'd lost. I'm so very sorry. It was selfish of me, and narrow-minded."

Erin looked at him in shock. When she didn't speak he pressed on.

"I had some information on you, you know, and your husband—but it wasn't nearly enough. I wanted to know exactly who had given birth to my son. I didn't hear about your family life or what happened after that until the night we took Riley to the emergency doctor." He lifted a hand to his face and rubbed his eyes. "It was a helluva night, wasn't it?"

"That's one way of describing it," she said tightly.

"Damn, I'm sorry. I don't mean to minimize what happened, what I did and said to you. I'd received confirmation that Riley was mine and I wanted to tell you. That day, out on the boat, it was the perfect opportunity, but then we got the call that Riley was sick. When you asked me to get the car keys, the last thing I expected to see on your desk was the letter from the laboratory confirming James wasn't Riley's dad—the date on the letter told me you had known for weeks.

"I have to admit, I saw red, but I couldn't challenge you with it there and then. We had to get Riley to the doctor."

"And then I made you drive," she commented.

"Yeah."

For an instant, that old shiver of apprehension rippled up his spine but he ignored it. He'd conquered that demon because she'd made him do it. If she hadn't, he might never have driven again. After the accident, his license had been suspended for six months and his lawyer had negotiated a period of probation for him so he hadn't served any time for his negligence. He'd never wanted to get behind the wheel again, ever. He'd wanted to continue to punish himself forever, if that was what it took to relieve the pain of what he'd done. And then he'd found Riley. Another human being who needed him and, in that moment, relied on him to do the right thing. It had changed everything.

Sam dragged in a deep breath before continuing. "While you were in with Riley I got another call from my investigator. One that told me about your life before you came to the lake."

She paled visibly. "I guessed as much," she said, wrapping her arms about her middle as if she could protect herself from what was to come. "I didn't exactly lead an exemplary life."

"You didn't exactly have the care and protection a child should have in their home prior to that either. You had nowhere else to go, did you?"

"Lots of people leave home and still make a go of things without getting into the trouble I did."

Sam felt the love in his heart swell even more when she didn't allow herself any excuses, but wasn't that part of the problem? That she was so hard on herself that she was prepared to give Riley up altogether?

"Can you tell me a bit about it?"

"What? My *happy* home life or what it was like living on the streets? To be honest with you, oblivion was better than either of them. You know it all anyway, why do you need to hear it from me?"

"Because I need to know it from your side."

He waited, silently urging her to carry on. Her gaze was focused intently on Riley as he rolled again on his mat, his attention suddenly riveted on a toy just out of his reach. Erin bent down and shifted the toy closer, letting Riley reach for and grab it himself. Finally, she sat back in her chair and began to speak.

"My mother never wanted me. She blamed me, incessantly, for my father leaving before I was born. We didn't have much while I was growing up and she liked to make sure that I knew that was my fault, too. At some point I realized that wasn't normal. That her bitterness toward me wasn't like what other kids' mommies were like with their families. I learned to hide when she was on a bender, to duck when her fists were a little too free."

Sam heard the understatement in her words. Fury against her mother fired to life inside him. If the woman couldn't provide the very basics of human comfort to her child, why then didn't she allow her to stay with someone who could? Every child deserved at least that, surely?

"As soon as I was old enough," Erin continued, "I left. I ended up with a brief stay in a foster home with a great family, but my mother fought to get me back—even now I can't understand why she did that unless it was to make sure my life was as utterly miserable as hers. I'd run away again, and got taken back a few times, but eventually I got smart enough not to be caught, and then my mother died and I somehow slipped off the radar.

"It was easier then, but I got into a few bad habits, made some bad choices."

"Tell me about the baby that died," he pressed.

She swallowed hard before speaking, her voice jerky as she recounted the story. "I didn't know the couple well. We were staying in an abandoned building, a bunch of us. People came and went, you didn't make friends. When a new couple showed up we were sur-

prised they had a baby girl with them. She can't have
been much more than a few months old. Seemed to me
that she was like the meat in the sandwich with her parents. If one was angry at the other they'd take it out on
her. Nothing too obvious, like hitting her or anything
like that—initially at least. It was more things like leaving her in a dirty diaper and blaming the other for not
changing her or for not buying diapers. Pinching her to
make her cry when the other was holding her. We all
saw what was going on." Erin's voice began to quake.
"I tried to help the mother when I could but he made
me stop."

"He?" Sam prompted.

"The father. He was small and wiry and liked to use
his fists to prove he was just as good as anyone who was
bigger than him. One night, he threatened me. Pushed
me face-first up against a wall, with my arm twisted
behind my back. He warned me not to interfere with
his family again or he'd kill me. No one would care, he
said. No one would know.

"I stayed well out of the way after that. One night,
I went out and met up with some other acquaintances.
Had a few too many to drink and I passed out. By the
time I woke up and went home the police were there.
The baby had been hurt really badly. We were all taken
in for questioning and the media had a field day with
us all. I know we weren't innocent. That little girl died
and I knew that any one of us should have stood up to
her parents, or called the authorities—something, anything, to protect that innocent child.

"I always thought my mother was a bad person, but I
was worse. I did nothing when I could have done something. I could have been that little girl's one chance to
have a better life—what am I saying? Even just a *life*—

if I'd only done something, spoken to *someone*. It was a heck of a wake-up call. I promised myself I'd clean up my act. The police never did get enough evidence on anyone to press charges. I vowed that if I ever had a baby, I would be the best mother it could ever have. I'd love it, I'd protect it—it would want for nothing. When I came here and met James it was like a dream come true. I wanted to create a perfect life for us. Too perfect for him, though. Eventually I drove him into another woman's arms."

Sam sat up straighter in his chair. "He was unfaithful to you?"

Erin wiped an errant tear from her cheek and nodded. "When I found out, we'd already entered the IVF lottery. I confronted him about it, asking him what he wanted. Us and the chance to have a family, or her. He chose us. But then he got sick and, well, you know the rest."

Sam felt as if he'd been through a wringer listening to her story—but she'd had it worse, she'd lived it. He knew there was more, so very much more. Layers and layers of hard times and hard choices. His respect for Erin grew in leaps and bounds, his love for her deepened. She'd gone through so very much and still come out determined to be the best person possible at the very end. It was no great wonder that after all she'd endured, she'd been prepared to conceal the truth about Riley's paternity in order to continue to keep the home that meant so much to her.

It wasn't just that she loved the lodge—although he knew she did. It was also because she knew exactly how hard it was for a young mother out there with nothing and no one to help her support her infant.

"You're an incredible woman, Erin Connell."

"No, I'm not."

"Look, I allowed my emotions to cloud my perspective where you were concerned. They made my reaction to hearing about your past just that, a reaction. With no thought, no consideration. I stand by my statement, Erin. You *are* incredible."

"Your emotions?" she looked up and stared at him.

"I was falling in love with you, Erin." To his horror she paled even further.

"And I screwed that up, too, didn't I?" she said brokenly.

"I'd thought—hoped—that maybe you were falling in love with me, too. Weren't you?"

Seventeen

Riley started to fuss on the mat and rubbed at his eyes with his pudgy little fists.

"It's time for his morning nap. I'll get his bottle."

Erin leaped to her feet and disappeared in the direction of the kitchen. She'd latched onto the chance not to answer his question and had all but run from the room. Had he read her all wrong after all? Had she not been falling in love with him? He scooped Riley up off the floor and cradled him in his arms.

"Sorry, my boy, I don't have the goods you're looking for right now."

She was back within a couple of minutes, a warmed bottle in her hand. She thrust it at him.

"Here, you may as well do it. You'll be doing a lot more of it soon, anyway."

Somehow, in the short time she'd been in the kitchen, she'd shored up her defenses again. The vulnerability that had been starkly visible on her face only moments ago was gone. He took the bottle from her and offered it to Riley, who dutifully opened his mouth and eagerly began to drink, his little hands slapping against the sides of the bottle and Sam's hand. It was a precious moment, but one that highlighted the gulf that was opening up between Erin and Riley.

"You're bottle feeding him now?" Sam asked without thinking.

"It's in the terms of the contract that he be weaned before you have full custody."

She said it bluntly, in a no-nonsense voice that almost managed to hide the longing in her voice. Guilt gave him a hard mental slap. Lost for words, he poured his attention into watching the boy in his arms. Riley was almost asleep by the time he finished the bottle.

"Do I still need to burp him?" Sam asked, confused as to what to do next. "Or will I wake him too much?"

Erin had always done everything so competently, and the size of the task ahead of him now began to assume enormous proportions. Sure, he'd have nannies around the clock, but even so, there was a lot he still needed to learn because he wanted to be a hands-on dad.

She rose and collected a cloth from a small stack on a nearby table and put it on his shoulder. "Don't worry, he won't wake."

After Riley had burped, Sam handed him over to Erin, who took him to his room to put him down in his crib.

"This is really hard for you," he said as she came back into the room.

"Talk about the understatement of the year."

"Why did you stop fighting?"

She gave him an incredulous look. "I beg your pardon?"

"Why did you stop fighting me, for custody of Riley?"

"I think that's self-explanatory, don't you?"

"On the face of things, yes. You're strapped for cash, you soon won't have the lodge to live in. But none of those things are insurmountable." He chose his next words very carefully, delivered them with great reluctance. But he wanted the most honest response she was capable of. "Why did you give up?"

Shock turned to fiery anger in her eyes, twin spots of color highlighted her cheeks and her hands fisted on the arms of the easy chair she had settled into.

"How dare you!"

"I dare because I need to know, Erin. Why did you give up?" he repeated the question, enunciating the words very slowly. Prodding her to respond.

"I had to do what was best for Riley."

"Are you saying you weren't already? Don't lie to me. I've seen the kind of mother you are—devoted to your last breath."

Pain scored her features. "That may be so, but it's not enough, is it? It doesn't put food on a table, clothes on a child's back, provide an education and opportunities in the world. Devoted doesn't always mean safe."

She got up from her chair and walked over to the montage of baby photos on the wall, lifting her finger to trace Riley's newborn features. "Don't you see? I may have given birth to him, but Riley's yours. You want him. You've fought for him. You will do whatever it takes to protect him and to provide for him. If you were any less of a father in your heart and your mind I would have fought you. You can be certain of that."

And suddenly Sam understood why she'd been prepared to sign the agreement uncontested. He was offering Riley what she'd been denied all her life. A loving parent, safety, security, a home. A future.

His heart swelled. He did offer all that to Riley, would give it unconditionally. But he wanted to give that to Erin, too. He got up to stand behind her and placed his hands on her shoulders, carefully turning her to face him. He could feel her bones through her shirt. He'd thought she looked drawn but it hadn't occurred to him that she'd lost so much weight. He would make it right. He would make everything right.

If only she'd let him.

"Erin, I asked you before, if you were falling in love with me. I'd like to think that you were."

"Why? So you can hold something else over my head? Destroy another piece of me? Don't bother. I'm not worth it."

Her voice was tight, as if it hurt to talk. She refused to meet his gaze and he could see the sheen of moisture in her eyes. Sure, he understood her hurt over his paternity claim, but her pain went so much further. Past giving up Riley. Past the baby who died in the squat house. Past the trouble she'd gotten into as a rebellious teen. All the way back to the little girl who'd grown up knowing her father hadn't cared enough to stick around and that her mother didn't love her.

"I misjudged you, Erin. It was a mistake, one I intend to rectify. You are everything I thought you were when I first met you. A loving and protective mother, and a capable and beautiful woman."

She started to shake her head but he caught her chin and gently tilted her face up to his.

"I began to fall in love with you the first moment I

saw you. I fought it—my God, I fought it. I'd been living in my own version of hell for so long I had convinced myself I didn't deserve to feel anything for anyone, ever again. When it came to the crunch, I'd only let them down again. But my heart wouldn't listen when I tried to tell myself you were off-limits.

"That night when you kissed me, it was everything I had dreamed of in a kiss. I knew I wanted more. I pushed you, even though I could see you were fighting your own battle with your attraction to me. I'd like to think that the first time we made love, it really was making love, and not just sex between us. I know it was for me. I love you, Erin Connell."

"No, you can't. I've been a bad person, I've done bad things. I tried to keep you from your own child. How can you possibly love me?"

He could hear what she wasn't saying. *How can you love me when I'm so unlovable?* Her father left her, her mother abandoned her emotionally. Even her husband couldn't stand by his marital vows to her. She'd had some hard knocks in her life, but no more. Provided she was willing—and if she wasn't he planned to somehow thoroughly convince her—he'd do everything in his power to make sure she endured no more hardships, no more loss.

"I love the woman I see before me. The Erin I know. The real you. I doubted myself and my judgment. I allowed my mind to be clouded by the information that was given to me about your past, without thinking about how hard you'd worked to put that all behind you. To become the person you always deserved to be.

"I am deeply sorry for everything I've put you through. You deserve better than that. Better than me. But I hope you'll give me another chance. Let me show you how much I love you, how much I admire your strength and who you've made yourself to be."

He heard her shocked gasp as he dropped to one knee.

"Erin, you showed me I can love again, that people are capable of change for good, even people like me who make terrible mistakes in their lives. You've made me a better man. A man who loves you with all his heart. Please, will you marry me? Will you be my wife, and Riley's mother, forever?"

Erin felt her knees buckle beneath her but she knew Sam would catch her and keep her safe. Not just now, but always.

"Are you sure?" she asked.

"I've never been more sure of anything," Sam confirmed.

One look at his face and she knew he was speaking the truth. Her heart began to swell and lift. The misery and pain of not just the past few weeks, but the past few years began to fade and something new edged in to take its place. Sam loved her. *Her!* She could barely believe it.

"I love you, Sam," she whispered, barely able to speak for the new sensation of joy that now spread through her.

He smiled back at her. That beautiful crooked, sweet smile that always made her heart flip.

"So, will you? Marry me?"

"Yes, I will. But not because you're Riley's father. I want you to be clear on that. I want to marry you because I love you with everything that's inside of me. I want to be your partner, your lover and your best friend for the rest of my life."

Sam's arms closed around her, holding her to his warmth, securing her against his heart.

"You need never worry about anything on your own, ever again, Erin. I will always be here for you. Always."

Erin lifted her lips to his, tasting his promise with the sure knowledge that she was loved and valued and that now she had a future, *they* had a future. All of them. Sam, Riley and her. Together. And she knew it would be long and happy, with Sam by her side.

* * * * *

A sneaky peek at next month...

MODERN™

INTERNATIONAL AFFAIRS, SEDUCTION & PASSION GUARANTEED

My wish list for next month's titles...

In stores from 21st June 2013:

☐ His Most Exquisite Conquest – Emma Darcy

☐ His Brand of Passion – Kate Hewitt

☐ The Couple who Fooled the World – Maisey Yates

☐ Proof of Their Sin – Dani Collins

☐ In Petrakis's Power – Maggie Cox

In stores from 5th July 2013:

☐ One Night Heir – Lucy Monroe

☐ The Return of Her Past – Lindsay Armstrong

☐ Gilded Secrets – Maureen Child

☐ Once is Never Enough – Mira Lyn Kelly

Available at WHSmith, Tesco, Asda, Eason, Amazon and Apple

Just can't wait?

0613/

The World of Mills & Boon®

There's a Mills & Boon® series that's perfect for you. We publish ten series and, with new titles every month, you never have to wait long for your favourite to come along.

Blaze®
Scorching hot, sexy reads
4 new stories every month

By Request
Relive the romance with the best of the best
9 new stories every month

Cherish™
Romance to melt the heart every time
12 new stories every month

Desire
Passionate and dramatic love stories
8 new stories every month

Join the Mills & Boon Book Club

Want to read more **Modern™** books?
We're offering you **2 more** absolutely **FREE!**

We'll also treat you to these fabulous extras:

- 🌹 **Exclusive offers and much more!**

- 🌹 **FREE home delivery**

- 🌹 **FREE books and gifts with our special rewards scheme**

Get your free books now!

visit www.millsandboon.co.uk/bookclub
or call Customer Relations on 020 8288 2888